THE WILD BOARS

Kosovo's dreamscapes and nightmares

by

P.I. KAPLLANI

THE WILD BOARS
Kosovo's dreamscapes and nightmares
By P.I. KAPLLANI

Published by: In Our Words Inc./www.inourwords.ca

Editors: Nina Munteanu
Cheryl Antao-Xavier
Brandon Pitts
Nick Bowman

Author photo: Sokol Papathimiu

Cover design: Sokol Papathimiu

Book design: Shirley Aguinaldo

Library and Archives Canada Cataloguing in Publication

Kapllani, Perparim, 1966-, author
The wild boars : Kosovo's dreamscapes and nightmares / P.I Kapllani.

Issued in print and electronic formats.
ISBN 978-1-926926-69-8 (hardback).--ISBN 978-1-926926-68-1 (paperback).--
ISBN 978-1-310-80909-5 (pdf)

1. Kosovo War, 1998-1999--Atrocities--Fiction. I. Title.

PS8621.A62W54 2016 C813'.6 C2016-903955-2
C2016-903956-0

DEDICATION

I dedicate this story to Dren Caka, formerly of Kosovo. In April 1999, while I was working as a journalist for *Shekulli* newspaper, I interviewed him and his father in the military hospital in Tirana. He was ten years old at the time. His tragic life story at that young age became the base for this work of fiction.

ACKNOWLEDGEMENTS

I want to thank Brandon Pitts for editing the original draft of this story, which was then titled "The Hunter." It was he who presented my manuscript to Quattro Books in 2015, where it was shortlisted from hundreds of submissions to be among the Top Six selections. This encouraged me to think seriously about rewriting the novel. Nina Munteanu, along with Cheryl Antao-Xavier were already there to put in significant editorial contributions. Word by word, sentence after sentence, together we achieved this extraordinary work of bringing to life my second novel in English. This is a huge achievement for me because my first language is Albanian.

Thank you IOWI, for making my dream of publication come true on the eve of my fiftieth birthday. Exactly three years earlier my first English novel *The Last Will* was published, also by IOWI.

I want to thank the actor Xhemi Agaj for his help in translating some sentences in the dialogue in the Serbian language.

Special thanks goes to Sokol Papathimiu for the wonderful cover design and e-book formatting and design and upload to the largest e-platform on the planet, Smashwords.com.

Big thank you to the Albanian Canadian Association, in particular to Mrs. Ruki Kondaj and Mr. Ramazan Kellezi for their ongoing support in the promotion of this book to a wider audience. I sincerely hope that together we succeed in making this amazing story that is based in an important time in our common histories widely known.

TABLE OF CONTENTS

FOREWORD

The Wild Boars is a fictional story about the life of the protagonist, Ermal Bllaca. Ermal is a ten-year-old boy, living with his family in the city of Gjakova, when a Serbian police patrol swarms through their neighbourhood identifying and massacring ethnic Albanians. The mass killings of civilians were conducted across Kosovo as part of the ethnic cleansing that followed in the wake of the NATO airstrikes of March 1999.

This fictional story mirrors the real life events of Dren Caka, who as a young boy fled from Serbian police along with thousands of other Albanians to neighbouring countries. I had the chance to meet Dren for the first time when as a journalist covering the plight of the refugees, I interviewed him at the military hospital where he was being treated for a bullet wound. Dren described to me how his mother and three sisters were killed by the Serbian Police. I want to thank him for being my inspiration to write *The Wild Boars*. I did not meet him again, even though he lives somewhere in Canada. Through my research I discovered that he had several times been called to The Hague as a witness against Slobodan Milosevic.

In this novel, the fictional Ermal grows up in Canada. His father moves on with his life, but the boy is consumed by thoughts of revenge and plots to hunt down and kill Spasic, his mother's killer. He tracks down Spasic in Serbia where he is a hunter of wild boar. The story unfolds as a plan for revenge that takes the reader from Canada to Serbia to Australia.

P.I. Kapllani

PREFACE

24 March 1999. A thousand NATO aircraft began operating from air bases in Germany and Italy. USS Theodore Roosevelt holder plane had just landed on the Adriatic Sea. Spanish Air Force Aircraft F/A-18 Hornets were the first to throw bombs on Belgrade. BGM - 109 Tomahawk began to fire missiles from ships and submarine, supported by a battalion of Apache helicopters which belonged to the Eleventh US Regiment Army Aviation. NATO airstrikes hit Belgrade's Ministry of Interior building, the Chinese embassy, and several bridges over the Danube River.

PART ONE

THE HORSESHOE

ONE

Someone was banging on the front door with what sounded like the butt of a gun. The knocks were forceful. Ermal Bllaca threw the blankets off and jumped out of bed. He opened the door of his room slightly and saw his father Adem get up, wiping his sleepy eyes with the back of his hand. His mom Valbona woke up too. She sat on the bed, trying to peer through the blinds over the window. Ermal's three sisters came out of their room, which was beside his, leaving the door wide open. Adem motioned to them to be quiet, put his jacket on and came out in his pyjamas. Valbona ran after him, grabbed his arm and tried to stop him. Her eyes were filled with fear. Adem squeezed her hand softly.

"Don't worry! I'll be back in a minute!" he said and opened the front door.

Ermal saw his father walking through the front yard and he couldn't stay behind. He ran after him as fast as he could, and reached him just as he opened the outside door. A police patrol was standing in front of the house. Ermal recognized the tension in his father's face, even as he pretended there was nothing to worry about. All three policemen had guns strapped to their shoulders. Ermal recognized the taller one who came closer. It was Dragan Spasic, his friend Nenad's father. He was their neighbour.

Ermal caught the smell of alcohol and almost vomited. He stepped back a little as Dragan Spasic took another step toward them. Ermal could see deep into his eyes where he noticed two little yellow fires. The retinas of his eyes resembled those of a wild wolf. There was hate and anger burning in those two little fires, something inhuman and frightful.

"*Çfarë ka ndodhur*?" Adem asked him in Albanian.

Dragan scowled. "We're going door to door to let people know that they don't have to leave their homes. Nothing bad is going to happen," Dragan said in an icy voice in Serbian.

Adem could tell it was a lie and was opposite to what the Serb really felt about them, his Albanian neighbours. If it was up to Dragan, he would send them straight to hell.

"*Hvala*," Adem mumbled in Serbian, shaking his head in obedience and humility. ("Thanks.")

Dragan squinted at them. He took a piece of chalk out of his pocket and marked Bllaca's front yard door with a big cross. He put the gun on his shoulder and was about to leave, but Adem kept staring at him.

"*Sta je*?" Dragan asked him in Serbian. ("What's up?")

"*Zasto si pisao na moja vrata*?" Adem replied in Serbian. ("Why did you write on my door?")

"*Hocu da znam ko je ovde shiftar*!" Dragan replied sharply. ("I want to know who is Albanian here!")

His answer left Adem speechless.

"You know who I am! I am your neighbour, *bre*!" Adem fired back.

"We have to identify all the Albanians in the neighbourhood." Dragan pointed to the other homes. He stared at Adem as if he wanted to chew him alive, and winked at the patrol to move to the next-door neighbour. Adem clenched his teeth tightly, forcing himself to stay quiet.

A military truck lumbered into the neighbourhood, drawing Ermal's attention. A crowd of Serbian neighbours milled around the truck. Two Serbian workers from the Post Office and three soldiers unloaded guns and started handing them over to their compatriots. It wasn't the first time that the Serbian army and the police gave guns to Serbian civilians. Father and son exchanged a glance. The police patrol left their home and stopped by the next-door neighbour, another Albanian family.

Dragan took the chalk out of his pocket again and marked the neighbour's door with a white cross. All the Albanian homes were marked that morning, one after another. The houses which were not marked belonged to the Serbs.

Even though Ermal was just ten years old, he felt that something big and ugly was about to happen. He had never seen the Serbian police go to every single Albanian home and tell them not to leave but marked their doors instead. Adem watched them and grabbed Ermal's arm, pulling him back into the house.

"Babi!" Ermal stared at his father. "Why are they marking our doors with white chalk?" Adem didn't answer, except to motion for him to enter the kitchen.

Ermal's mother was sitting at the kitchen table with a forced smile on her face to make them feel at ease, but it didn't hide her anxiety. Ermal's fourteen-year-old sister Hana stood beside her, clutching the back of her mother's chair. Six-year-old Trëndelina shivered beside her, holding her sister's hand. The youngest daughter, Diona, was only two years old and was still in her bed.

Valbona waited for her husband to say something. Adem swallowed.

"Why are all of you here? Go back to sleep," Adem said. None of them moved.

"What did the policemen say? What did they want so early in the morning?" Valbona looked at him intensely, eyes filled with fear.

"They said not to worry about anything and not to leave our homes." Adem went straight to the living room. He didn't tell her the most important detail, that their home was marked with chalk by Serbian police.

Ermal kept quiet. He felt that Babi didn't want to create panic. Babi looked lost in thought as he pushed the burning logs further into the fire with a pair of tongs, causing sparks to climb up the chimney. Ermal's two older sisters followed Babi's order and went back to their room. Ermal grabbed a soccer ball and bounced it on the floor a few times. He didn't understand why the police marked their door. He didn't see any reason to worry since their family had nothing to do with the Kosovo Liberation Army. They were just an ordinary Albanian family minding their own business. Their routine was *hanging on for survival,* as Mami said.

"Babi, can I go and play soccer?" Ermal asked him shyly. He could read the pain on his Babi's face caused by his innocent request. His world was far from his. He couldn't even imagine that he would soon be missing even a simple soccer match in the streets of his neighbourhood.

"Not right now. Maybe later on in the afternoon. Eat breakfast first." He ruffled the boy's hair.

Valbona came to stand beside her husband. "I don't trust one word the police say. We better pack everything and leave. That's all they want: to keep us here so they can kill us!"

"Let's wait and see," Adem replied and came closer to the window as the first rays of the morning sun penetrated through the blinds.

* * * *

Later that afternoon, Ermal was playing soccer with his Serbian childhood friend, Nenad; Adem Bllaca had felt it safe enough to let his son go out to play.

Nenad kicked the soccer ball as hard as he could, sending it straight to the left corner. Ermal leapt up with all his strength to stop it. He barely touched the ball with the tips of his fingers, unable to deviate its trajectory, and it slid into the net.

Ermal fell on the field. He didn't get up, staring to the far side of the field toward Milos Gilica Street. Nenad laughed and shook the dust off his pants. Then, alerted, he turned to where Ermal was staring.

A policeman stood there, watching the two boys play. He'd probably been there for several minutes. He looked big and angry. He had a moustache cut really short and a very big nose. Ermal recognized him right away. It was the same policeman who marked their door that morning: Dragan Spasic, a police officer at Gjakova Police Station. Nenad's father.

Their homes were located on the same street, not far from each other in the neighbourhood of Qerim, and Ermal had seen Nenad's father in his police uniform several times when he was going to and from work. Nenad also had a sister, a year older than him, Slavica, who used to come and watch them play in the school field.

Dragan approached Nenad, stomping on the grass like he wanted to grind it into the ground with his weight, which was probably more than two hundred pounds. He yelled, "*Koliko puta sam ti reko da ne igras sa Shiftarama*?" ("How many times have I told you not to play with *Shiptars*?") "Shiptars" was the word used by the Serbs for the Albanians. The Albanians called themselves *Shqiptarë*, but the Serbs were pronouncing it without the "q" in the middle, giving the word a bad connotation, stressing their belief that the Albanians were second-class citizens.

"*Dodji kući, sada je mrak*!" he said. ("Come home. It's getting dark.") He pulled Nenad by his arm, scowling at Ermal.

Nenad waved at him then followed his father, looking downcast. Ermal couldn't understand why Nenad's Babi didn't like them. Nenad and he were close friends. When they played soccer, Slavica used to come with them, watching Ermal with her blue eyes. Nenad and Slavica couldn't speak Albanian, but for Ermal that wasn't a problem, since Albanians were forced to learn Serbian in elementary school. Ermal dreamt of her beautiful face. Her blue eyes filled with love and her curly hair would blow in the wind. Slavica became his dream girl, but he struggled to hide his feelings and bury them in his heart, saying to himself that he was still too young and it was shameful to think about those things. He took the soccer ball in his hands and headed home, looking back a few times to see if Slavica was watching him from behind the curtains. He didn't see her.

As he approached his house, Ermal noticed that the neighbourhood wasn't as noisy as it normally was. The streets were unusually empty.

A sudden roar accompanied a long row of army trucks and police cars down the main road. He ran to the front door of his home and rapped on the door, then waited for his mother to let him in. He heard her steps approach, accompanied by a set of lighter steps that created a rhythmic melody to his ear, as if they were stepping on cobblestones. He heard a sudden childish laugh behind the door. As soon as his mother opened it, his second sister Trëndelina jumped into his arms. His mother caressed his hair and kissed him on the cheek. Ermal sighed and went inside, feeling relieved.

TWO

It was eight o'clock in the evening when Adem heard the wolves howling. He jumped off his chair in the living room and stepped to the window. He didn't see anything. Milos Gilica Street was deserted. His wife Valbona froze, holding a basket in her hand filled with slices of homemade bread. Hana rushed to stand behind Adem, craning to see what was happening. Diona woke and started to cry in her cradle. Adem went over to her and lifted her in his arms to stop her crying. He kissed Diona on her forehead and sat beside the others at the dinner table. Valbona's hands were shaking as she placed the basket on the table. Adem pretended not to see her shaking.

"I heard the wolves howling," Valbona whispered. She took a slice of bread and brushed it with butter. The bread was still warm from the oven. Valbona used to make bread herself and rarely bought from the nearby bakery. The smell of freshly baked bread spread all over the house.

With the youngest daughter in his arms, Adem got up from the table and shut off the lights. They still could see because of the dim light coming from the fireplace.

* * * *

Ermal couldn't sleep that night because of the sound of the wolves. The winter had not ended yet and it was still cold. The Accursed Mountains were still white. The thick layer of frozen snow hadn't gotten any lower. The hungry wolves were leaving the forests and attacking the cities and villages of Kosovo.

Ermal had never read about wolves coming so close to homes looking for food. Even though he didn't know how to pray, he closed his eyes and prayed to God for the very first time in his life.

Dear God, you probably have eyes and ears to listen to my prayers; please save us from this danger. It will be too late tomorrow, so please listen to my prayers today.

Ermal still couldn't sleep. He finally got up and opened the door. He crept to his parents' room and settled quietly by the door. It was halfway open. He glimpsed Babi's face, looking mysterious in the dark. Mami's face was a frozen statue. He could hear their urgent whispers.

The Albanians say that even the walls have ears, which is why they say the most important things to each other in a very low voice.

"What should we do?" she asked Babi. "We can't stay here any longer, pretending that nothing is happening. They will storm our door and cut us into a thousand little pieces," Mami said in a shaking voice.

"I'll do something," Babi said reassuringly and got up from the bed. In a matter of seconds, he opened the door right in Ermal's face. The boy felt ashamed that he was caught listening to them, but he didn't move.

"What the hell are you doing here?" Babi asked, trying to be mad at him. But it didn't work. Babi sighed with pain in his heart. He hugged his son and kissed him on the forehead. "Go sleep, son," he said.

"I can't."

Mami got up from her bed. She joined them and looked toward the front door.

"What are you going to do about it?" she asked Babi.

"I'm going to park the car right in front of our gate," Adem replied.

He opened the front door and walked into the front yard. The gate was almost ten meters away from the front door. Ermal tiptoed after him, keeping quiet. Babi loosened the heavy chain from the front yard gate and looked outside. His Golf was parked on the side of the road. Adem checked in both directions. There was no one there. He got into his car and parked it right in front of the entrance to the house, blocking the gate to the front yard with its width. He got out and stood in front of the house for several minutes.

Babi still felt unsafe. He noticed Ermal and "sh-sh-shushed" him with a finger on his lips and walked the inner perimeter of the surrounding wall. Ermal followed him again, this time much closer, only a couple of steps away. The boundary wall was built with red bricks and was almost two meters above ground.

When they reached the backyard, Adem noticed a man on top of the roof of their next-door neighbour's house. That home belonged to Arben Morina, Adem's first cousin. Adem pretended not to see him, but the shadow on top of the roof waved at them. Adem grabbed Ermal's arm and pulled him closer, like he wanted to protect his only son from something dangerous, then finally decided to respond to the shadow on the roof. Even in the dark, Ermal noticed Arben's thick eyebrows.

"What are you doing up there?" Adem asked Arben.

"I've been watching the army howling like wolves. This is the end!"

"That might be real wolves," Adem said, pointing at Ermal. Arben studied the little boy from the roof and got the message that Adem didn't want to scare the child.

"You never know! You're damn right. They might be! The humans became wolves and the wolves are behaving like humans."

"What did they look like?" Adem asked him.

"They had the same snout as beasts do. The same nails. Even their ears were long and hairy, just like wolves. Their skin was covered with a lot of hair."

"Are you serious?"

"You think I'm joking?"

"Did they speak like humans?"

"They're giving military orders in Serbian."

"Did they have tails?"

"Maybe. I was too far to see everything in detail. They probably stuck their tails in their pants. We better leave from here as fast as we can, otherwise it's going to be too late for all of us. Take your family and hide somewhere. That is what I'm going to do."

Ermal didn't believe Arben's tale, but something in his mind told him that Arben was right about one thing: they had to leave immediately. Ermal's face contorted with fear and sorrow.

Arben jumped off the roof and walked toward them. Ermal could see his face more clearly. It was strained with lines of anxiety.

"How are you, big boy?" Arben shook his hand, pretending

that Ermal was a real big man. "You grew up so fast!" He forced a smile on his face.

Ermal didn't speak. He was already feeling sorry for Arben and scared for all of them. His throat was dry. Adem saluted Arben and ushered Ermal back into the house as Arben returned to his.

Valbona was waiting for them at the door. The question in her eyes was what to do next. Adem avoided her for the moment, but her eyes followed him inside the house. Her voice sounded weak, like she was begging for something with all her soul. "Why don't you talk, Adem? What are we going to do?" she asked him desperately.

"I'm still thinking. I have to find a safe place for all of you. Tonight we are not going anywhere. The kids have to sleep. Tomorrow is another day. We'll wait and see."

Valbona shook her head in despair. Her face darkened.

Adem knew that his answer did not satisfy his wife. Ermal knew that it was still winter and it was too cold outside. He guessed that Babi didn't have a clue where his four kids would take refuge in the middle of the night.

Adem shivered. There was no safe place for Albanians. He sat beside the fire, staring at the flames as if they would give him an answer.

Ermal could see a light of hope fire his Babi's eyes. It looked like two people inside Babi were struggling with each other deep in his subconscious.

"We have to follow the other Albanian families," Adem said. "KLA and NATO will do something to protect us from these beasts. We are not just pieces of meat up for grabs and we will not be alone in our misery. We are just minding our own business and we don't bother anyone. We should think of what will happen to us in case of war. We should have left a long time ago, not now. Let's go to sleep. We can decide tomorrow what to do." Adem then went to his room.

Adem got in his bed, but still couldn't sleep. He could hear the soldiers howling like wolves in the darkness. He felt so sorry for himself and his family. What the Serbian soldiers were doing was a disgrace to humanity. Their voices were heard sometimes in chorus, and at other times a solo howl would pierce the night. He had the impression that the howling had turned into a competition of which Serbian soldier could howl louder and convincingly.

After an hour or so the soldiers stopped howling. The four kids fell asleep, but not Adem. He got up from his bed, and walked to the window. He watched the road for a while for any sudden movement by the Serbian army and police. Then he went to bed, forcing himself to sleep, but he couldn't. The brief silence terrified him more than the howling.

THREE

A convoy of Serb M-84A tanks entered the Qerim neighbourhood. The weight of their metal treads mercilessly ground into the asphalt, which was wet with morning dew. The nearly eighty thousand inhabitants of the town of Gjakova lived in dread of their arrival.

Each of the twenty tanks had a 125-millimeter cannon, capable of opening fire at a rate of eight shells per minute. In the first tank, a wolfish-looking soldier carried a 7.62 millimeter automatic gun on his shoulder, his finger poised on the trigger. He swung the gun to aim at anything that moved on either side of the road. A top-caliber 12.7 millimeter antiaircraft gun sat atop the rotary tower tank. The heads of three 'wolves' protruded from each tank. In the lead tank, the stocky one on the right would be the tank commander, to the left was the sniper wolf, and between the two was the driver. The driver was constantly changing gears.

The wolves looked different from each other. The wolf on the left was tall and grey. The wolf on the right was the Cynodictis type, which was more like a fox and known as "the wolf of the dawn." He had long arms and gave the impression that at any moment he would scale a tree. The wolf behind the wheel had reddish skin and was smaller in build. The wolf on the left seat looked tall and burly. His head was larger than the grey wolf's.

Adem Bllaca peered out the window and bleakly watched the approach of the convoy of tanks. He wondered how such a thing could happen. Wild animals of the forest were wearing military uniforms and prowling through their city. He trembled, but continued to watch.

The Bllaca home was right at the entrance of the road and was the first to fall prey to the attack. The first tank came to a full stop after it crushed Adem's Golf under its thick chains. Adem had parked the Golf in front of their gate the night before. The convoy went roaring down the road, crushing and smashing whatever was in its way.

His older daughter Hana wept silently, while little Trëndelina trembled even though she did not understand what was going on. The six of them dressed quickly. Valbona grabbed a suitcase and threw in whatever she could find that would be useful for their sudden departure: underwear, socks, three wool sweaters and two towels. In less than five minutes they were outside in a cobblestoned alley behind the house. Adem checked both directions before they entered the lane.

"Do not make any noise," he whispered and led them toward Arben Morina's bungalow, which was an old brick building.

Two cypress trees were planted in front of the house, which always gave him the impression that they were perpetually guarding the gate. The fence of the house was covered with colourful format papers in yellow, red and black. More format papers hung on the top of the pickets and created a bizarre contrast with the other Albanian homes.

Adem raised the iron handle of the gate and knocked hard four times with an interval of five seconds between each knock.

Arben opened the door immediately and ushered Adem and his frightened family inside. White cheesecloth hung in the main plank porch, wrapped around freshly baked bread that smelled so irresistible. A wreath with dried garlic hung beside it and a horseshoe was nailed above the door.

Arben's father, Bajram, was sitting by the fire. He was in his eighties and almost deaf. He wore a white fez and worked prayer beads in his tired, wrinkled fingers. Adem wondered where Arben's kids and wife were. They were probably hiding somewhere already. The elder embraced the kids one by one, shook hands with Adem and Valbona and invited them to sit beside the fireplace. He held a cigarette paper between two fingers and pressed in some chopped tobacco, which was grown by Arben himself in their field on the mountain. He managed to leisurely roll a thin cigarette and compressed it well, but didn't light it, acknowledging that it wouldn't be appropriate to smoke in their guests' presence.

"Time has come for us to leave!" Adem said to Bajram.

"I can't hear you. What did you just say?" the old man complained and cupped his hand behind his ear.

"We have to leave now, before it's too late," Adem spoke slowly.

The elder shook his head in despair, while Arben brought out a cup of coffee and some tea for Valbona and the kids.

"I'll not leave. I'll wait right here for Judgment Day to come," the elder announced and kept counting on the *taspie*—the thirty-three little prayer beads. That number corresponded to the thirty-three of the ninety-nine different names of God. "Will God remember that He has to save us?" He looked upward.

Adem did not answer but saluted him and sipped his coffee. The hot drink took away his inertia and weakness without removing the frown on his face. It was one of the only peaceful moments of that day which he was to remember for a very long time.

"Where are the kids?" Adem asked Arben.

"I took them into the basement under the pool beside Sulejman Toplica's home," Arben said softly.

"Is there space for my family as well?" Adem asked him suddenly.

"Yes, of course! We'll take them there as soon as it gets a little dark. Then both of us can join the other men in the woods," said Arben.

The old man coughed heavily and pointed to the window.

"There are many dead all over Gjakova and elsewhere in Kosovo," Bajram said. "Souls of our people are wandering the streets. We Albanians have an old tradition. When our people die, we bury them with either a gun, a hook, or a fire tong. The iron keeps the evil away. Any kind of tool is good for that purpose: even a shovel or a mattock will stop evil from taking over the dead bodies. No ghost can get into the body of the deceased if there is a tool buried in the grave. The grave has to be watched over for three days so the ghosts can be scared off."

"What are those colourful papers stuck on top of the fence?" Adem asked him.

"They are for the vampires. How do we call them, son?" he asked Ermal.

"I have no idea," Ermal replied.

"We call them *lugat* in our language. So what they do, it's simple. They come here and attack us. They grab a piece of paper, bite the bread and smell the garlic. As for the horseshoe, I put it up there just for good luck."

"I know only one way to communicate with these vampires who are wearing military uniforms: shoot them with your gun!" Arben added.

Bajram Morina shook his head in approval. With all the weight of age on his back, he slowly rose from the corner of the chimney and pulled the Mauser gun from where it was hanging on the wall. With trembling hands, he pulled the bolt back and let it go free with a dry metallic click. The Mauser was shiny and spotless, oiled a day earlier by Arben. Bajram ambled to an old and heavy suitcase and took out a cartridge with bullets. He touched the bullets with his wrinkled fingers one by one, while his eyes shone with a secret fire. It seemed that just touching the gun was enough to make him feel twenty years younger.

"This rifle is a souvenir from my father," said Bajram. "He got it from his father. It's in your hands now, inherited generation after generation. I am afraid no spoken word will stop them, so we have no choice but to use this. I wish balls of fire would fall from heaven and burn them to ashes."

"I pray the NATO forces come in and stop them before it's too late," Arben said.

"We have to do something," said the old man and pointed the rifle toward the window. He held his breath and turned off the safety. His index finger was trembling slightly. He pulled the trigger, but nothing happened. The magazine was empty. The imaginary enemy was somewhere nearby, but could not be seen from there. Arben went to him and put his hand on the Mauser. The elder refused to let it go.

"Son, we have twenty bullets. We can kill twenty wolves," said the old man. His hands were trembling because of his high blood pressure. Stains on the tips of his fingers and on his face were caused by his heavy smoking. His hands were so wrinkled they looked like two big chunks of wood fallen off a hundred-year-old oak tree. He had worked hard all his life and had seven grown children. According to him, his wish was that "from all his kids, at least one would manage to stay alive." The old man had five boys and two girls. Some had been killed by Serbs, others by cold and hunger. Arsim was the oldest and he had been a soldier in the Yugoslav army. He came back home in a coffin. The official version from the Serbian army was that Arsim had killed himself, but when his parents opened the casket they found bruises all over his body. There were too many accounts of Albanian soldiers who committed suicide in the Yugoslav army in a short period of time. Arben was the only one of his sons left alive.

"Arben, you have to leave. Take Adem with you and hide somewhere. I swear I'll not waste the bullets. They will go straight to the foreheads of those blaggards," the old man said.

"Babi..."

"Do as I say!"

There was silence. It was an Albanian custom never to oppose your father. Babi speaks only once. And that was what Arben did. He kept his mouth shut. The elder hung the weapon back on the wall and sat beside the chimney. Arben and Adem stood frozen, looking at each other. The conversation was over. The elder had decided once and for all and nothing would change his mind. Arben sat down beside the old man looking desperate. Adem was overwhelmed by emotion and did not say anything.

"It's a very simple plan we have to follow. You have to hide the kids inside the basement below the pool and go yourself and hide somewhere. If the Serbs attack the pool, I'll shoot them from here. Do you hear what I say?"

"Yes, Babi! I hear you," Arben said and hugged his father.

FOUR

Sulejman Toplica's house was somewhat isolated from the others. The landlord had built a pool next to it which had a basement underneath. Some of Arben's relatives had taken shelter in the basement. It was isolated from the main road and gave the impression that the Serbian army or even pedestrians would not search the pool area since it was still winter and very late in the evening. It was the perfect spot for the women and children to hide.

Ermal shuddered from the cold. Although he was wearing a winter jacket, he felt the March wind-chill through his bones as he walked along the road to the shelter. He looked up at the window and saw Arben's father peering down at them. The old man's eyes followed their every step as they went towards the basement.

Hana and Trëndelina were dressed warmly, but still shivered from the cold. Valbona followed them, clutching her youngest daughter Diona in her arms. Adem hastened his steps, walking ahead of everyone. Arben brought up the rear of the little group, looking left and right for any surprise attacks. They arrived at the pool in a few minutes. Arben went down the stairs first and knocked on the door four times in short intervals. No one answered. He was about to knock again when the door opened.

Arben smiled when his wife Mimoza and his two little daughters appeared at the entrance. The youngest daughter Floria jumped into his arms and kissed him on the cheek as if she had not seen her Babi in a long time. They had spent only one night in the basement and the faces of both girls were pale. Arben began to count silently. Fifteen people were crammed inside that narrow basement, five women and ten children.

Arben noticed that Adem's eyes were brimming with tears. He had never seen his cousin cry. He patted him on the shoulder. Adem kissed Ermal on his forehead. "I'll see you soon," he said and turned his back.

"Babi, where are you going?" Ermal asked him, suddenly anxious.

"I'm going to guard outside. You take care of them inside here, okay? I think you can do this," Adem said.

Ermal nodded. Adem smiled and made for the door, but Hana and Trëndelina clung to him. Ermal watched his father hug them back then struggle to free himself and open the door. Then he left and closed it behind him. The rigid bar clanked as Valbona pivoted it into place, and then there was silence. Ermal imagined his Babi watching outside in the darkness and felt safe for a moment. It was somewhat quiet in the basement, except for whispering and crying of the babies. There were occasional sounds of bombing and anti-aircraft artillery. The explosions echoed from somewhere in the distance, as if it was happening in another world.

✻ ✻ ✻ ✻

The women and children spent more than four days in the basement, sitting around in the light of a kerosene lamp. Hardly anyone slept. The basement was a bit tight for the number of people huddled there. The underground hall served as a changing room in peacetime, whenever the neighbourhood children went swimming in the pool. Ermal felt sadness in his soul as he recalled those hot days of summer. The whole family used to come here at the peak of the heat, change their clothes quickly and eagerly jump into the cool water. It was early April and he had never thought that he would be coming to the pool this far ahead of summer.

Ermal looked around and saw that all of them were squeezed against each other and covered with woolen rugs that the women had brought with them. His mother had placed a cotton blanket over him and put a woolen sheepskin under his feet.

As time passed, Ermal recognized some of the kids in the basement. A strange feeling of fear gripped him. He did not understand why the kids and the women had to gather in a basement, but didn't complain to his mother, since it was the decision of their fathers. *Adults always know what to do.* That was what he thought until a powerful explosion sounded close to the pool area. Valbona instinctively stretched her hands toward her son to protect him from the unknown. Ermal felt safer in her arms.

He tried to nap. With eyes closed, his mind wandered. He saw himself on a soccer field. It was morning and he was a bit cold. In the corner of the field he caught sight of Nenad, who was laughing loudly. Nenad kicked the ball and Ermal jumped high above the net to catch it. When he caught the ball with both hands, he noticed that the ball was actually the severed head of a man. Ermal cried out in fear and opened his eyes. Thankfully it was a dream.

Valbona put her slender fingers through his hair. "Sleep, son," she whispered in his ear, but Ermal couldn't sleep. He had a bad feeling that the Serbian army or police would storm their safe haven any minute.

Valbona took out a pack of sleeping pills from her purse and gave one to him. The little package of Valium was passed to all the women, who gave their kids a pill to swallow. Ermal saw his two cousins, Floria and Shpresa, biting the pill with their little teeth, and then his eyelids became heavy. He lay his head on his mother's lap. He saw himself surrounded by a thick fog and noticed that the rest of the kids had fallen asleep. He was the only one who was still awake.

The women finally felt free to talk.

"The Serbs killed fourteen people at the bus stop," said one of the women, her voice racked from sobbing.

"Five Albanians were killed in the morning as they were trying to leave the city," his mother said in a low voice.

Ermal struggled to catch every word, but the pill made him drowsy.

FIVE

Bajram Morina supported the Mauser gun on his shoulder and aimed at the target outside, then pulled back immediately. The white *qeleshe* ("fez") on top of his head might be seen by Serbian snipers, so he took it off and then continued to watch the front yard. It was too dark to see anything, but he could clearly make out the tanks and armored vehicles rumbling in. *I must take each shot separately. If I do well, I have to remember how I did it and do it again. If I do not hit the target, I have to rethink, concentrate and try again.*

The old man sighted his rifle. He knew his Mauser well enough to have a perfect shot, but he had to control his finger on the trigger. Sighting the first tank of the convoy, he applied a steady pressure until the trigger broke. The shot surprised him—cracking in the dawn air—as he was still concentrating on the sight focus. Had he missed? He couldn't tell. He held his breath for an instant before taking the second shot. Even the slightest movement could move his shot off-target. He followed through with the second shot, not dropping the rifle after pulling the trigger. He couldn't tell if he'd hit his mark. His hands shook from age, so he lowered the gun and crouched down from the window to take a break.

He thought of Tahir Meha who was killed by Serbian forces in 1983, in his home along with his father. Tahir was surrounded in his *Kulla,* with his two wives and three daughters. He had killed eleven Serbian militiamen and when the tank stormed the front door, he jumped on it and threw a hand grenade inside the armored vehicle and tried to escape. Tahir was shot two hundred meters away by a helicopter, his arms were crushed by another tank, and he gave his last breath in an open field, facing the sky with his eyes wide open. *What a noble man he was! If I was his age, I would beat the hell out of them! The national hero of Kosovo, Adem Jashari was inspired by Tahir Meha. A group of KLA fighters along with twenty-six-year-old Adem appeared for the first time in military uniforms at Tahir Meha's funeral, and Adem swore on his dead hero's body that he was going to fight until Kosovo was free. That was the first time that the Kosovo Liberation Army had appeared in the public eye.*

The old man shook his head as if to get rid of those glorious memories and concentrate on his next target. Three army trucks loaded with policemen were bringing new reinforcements to the troops, which had already cordoned off the *Kulla* in an armoured siege. They had stomped out an area for themselves in a secluded part of the neighbourhood. The Army Special Units were coming closer to the house, crawling slowly toward it.

Bajram could hear the army trucks approach. There were two rooms on the third floor of the *Kulla*, several with windows facing the road. Bajram ran from room to room, shooting from every window, one after another, to give the approaching army and police the impression that they were dealing with many armed Albanians and not just one old man. It was still too dark to see anything and he wished the morning could come soon, so the whole area could be seen. He imagined his son Arben and his nephew Adem hiding on top of the roof of Sulejman Toplica's house.

Both men should have escaped the Serbian soldiers. They were probably hiding in the back of the building or they had jumped into the next door neighbour's backyard.

If I keep shooting from every single window, the policemen will think that there are many of us in the Kulla and so they will waste a lot of time with me here. This way I will give Arben and Adem the chance to jump from the roof and run toward the woods. They will contact the KLA soldiers in the forest for sure. Today the Big Wedding Day has come and, as we say, there is no wedding without meat.

He crept along the wooden floor to the other side of the room. He took position and aimed out the window. He held his breath and waited with his finger on the trigger, until he noticed smoke coming out of the barrel.

A hand grenade sailed through the window of the second floor. A huge explosion sounded and the front wall of the *Kulla* fell apart. The old man pulled the trigger slowly, taking his time for every single shot. A Serbian policeman fell to the ground, screaming with pain. *The fourth policeman down! There is no police, nor army, who can expel the Albanians from their lands. No way! Vaso Cubrilovic wrote all kinds of theories about the expulsion of the Albanians, but we are still alive and here we shall be!*

As he readied himself to shoot the next round, he felt a sharp pain on his left shoulder. He touched it with the tips of his fingers, and saw them stained with blood. He felt a sudden weakness and his view darkened. He could not see if Arben and Adem were still on top of Sulejman Toplica's roof. It sounded too good to be true that both of them had escaped the armoured siege.

Oh! Did they really leave or are they still on the rooftop? If they didn't make it, they will be killed. They will never make it to the woods. I've got to stay put and aim at the target very carefully and not waste any bullets. I must have bullets to hold them off a bit longer.

He clenched his teeth until they were grinding and got to his feet. He aimed at his next target. It was still too dark to see clearly. He placed the cartridge on its nest and a sweet feeling came over his body. He pulled the trigger and heard a scream and swearing in Serbian. As he made himself ready to shoot again, the three-story building he was in shook with a huge explosion. Bajram fell to the floor. The room filled with smoke and fire. Stones from the side-wall flew over his head. His face was covered by dust and the air choked him.

They hit the Kulla with tank shells! The Kulla is falling down on me. Let it be that way! This is the most beautiful day of my life! Is there any more meaningful day than this one, dying protecting my threshold? If this is God's will, I am ready to fight and die protecting my Kulla. The Serbian occupiers will take me out of here only after I am dead. Kulla is my last destination. It was built by my grandfather. Four generations have grown up in here.

His thoughts were interrupted by another tank shell. It hit the second floor. The whole triplex building shook and felt like the *Kulla* was giving its last breath. He suddenly felt something wet dropping down his wrinkled face. He touched his face with the tips of his fingers and felt the wetness of his own blood. A bullet had grazed his left cheek without causing a deep wound.

I feel that both of them have already escaped. God from above is telling me that my son Arben and his cousin Adem are safe. I see how they run on the road to freedom. All this concentration of forces here means that Serbian Army at this very moment is dealing only with me. After they are done with me, where are they going to? Eh?! Hopefully with God's will they will not think to look at the pool's basement. Even if they find them, they won't kill women and children. May God help those innocents.

He craved tobacco. The spray of bullets continued over him as he crouched under the window sill, unable to do anything. He took the pipe out from his pocket and lit it. The smoke of the minced tobacco relieved his pain. He placed a hand on the floor and got up and looked through the window.

"Let's get the party going," he shouted and put the *qeleshe* back on his head. The fez made him feel complete. His initial fear of the snipers dispersed. With the *Kulla* falling, there was nothing left to worry about.

"Po e pyet Sharri Drenicën/, ku e kam Azem Galicën?" ("Sharr is asking Drenica/, Where is Azem Galica?") He started to sing the song written for Azem Galica, a hero of Kosovo who fought all his life against the Serbian occupation, along with his wife Shota.

Bajram's loud voice echoed from the rubble and for a moment the gunfire stopped. It seemed as if the Serbian militants were listening to the old man singing. *"Në çdo lis e në çdo gur/ Os, len me vdek Kosova kurr."* ("In every oak tree, in every stone, He never let Kosovo be gone.") *"O prite Azem Galicën!"* ("Take this shot from Azem Galica!")

SIX

A volley of bullets ripped through the dark cloak of night. Arben Morina and Adem Bllaca checked the area and noticed an army truck parked in front of the pool. Policemen in camouflage uniforms patrolled the pathways between homes with their fingers hooked over the triggers of their guns. Most of them wore masks. Every five to ten minutes single shots rang out, giving the impression that the policemen were shooting at everything that moved in case it was an Albanian lurking behind a house or tree or fence.

The cousins crawled a few meters and a spray of bullets whistled over their heads. Both men lay on the ground, wet with the night dew, and remained still until the police crews and the army truck started to move away towards the heart of the neighbourhood. Arben lifted his head slightly, looking toward his home. Occasionally they spotted the fire off Bajram's barrel appearing at the two windows of the third floor. The single shots brought on a storm of Serbian gunfire.

"He shot six times so far," said Arben in a trembling voice, slightly out of breath. "Babi has only fifteen rounds left in the cartridge! I have to get into the building and save my father!" Tears stained his cheeks. "I should have never left my Babi in such a dangerous situation, abandoning him in there to die."

Adem gripped him like pliers tightening around his right arm. Arben shook him off and lurched toward the building. Adem challenged, "Your intent might be great, but you simply can't do it. Neither of us has a weapon. What can we do about it?"

"It's not right to let Babi die alone," Arben said emotionally. "You don't have to follow me. I can go ahead by myself!"

A huge blast echoed into the night and tongues of fire curled up toward the second floor of the *Kulla*. A tank shell had already penetrated the building, demolishing a large part of the left sidewall. Arben didn't stop. Adem watched him crawl slowly toward the building, eyes tracking in all directions. Arben pointed to the Mauser barrel vomiting fire from the third floor of the house once again.

"There are fourteen more bullets left," he whispered to Adem and resumed his crawl, then stopped suddenly. He touched his foot and drew back a hand covered in blood. "Ahh! I think a bullet hit me on my left foot," he said, glancing back. Adem pulled him back by the shoulders and dragged him to hide in the backyard of the closest abandoned home.

Arden's mouth went a little slack, as he struggled to keep his eyes open. Adem tore his shirt off and tied it around Arben's wound. Arben shut his eyes tight and yelped.

"Don't talk. I'll carry you on my shoulders and we'll get the hell out from here," Adem said. Arben looked back at his home, which was already on fire. A single shot echoed from the Mauser gun.

"Thirteen more bullets! *Baca* ("Babi") is still alive," Arben rejoiced in a hoarse voice, obvious pride that the old man was still standing his position. Then he fell unconscious, dropping his full weight on Adem.

* * * *

Arben lost all sense of time. His wounded foot was numb. The whole world swirled around him. He opened his eyes and licked his dry lips with the tip of his tongue. He noticed that Adem was carrying him on his shoulders and hurrying from one house to another.

"Adem, what happened to my father?" he asked hoarsely, but Adem was breathing with difficulty and didn't respond. He struggled to keep his balance, bending a little and looking around to ensure they weren't noticed by the militants. Arben realized that his cousin simply couldn't answer him. He felt sorry for him and just patted him a little on the shoulder, to show his gratitude for what Adem was doing for him. They eventually reached a house that had been burned down a few days ago. Smoke was still curling out from the blackened studs. Adem bent down with a grunt and laid Arben gently on the ground.

SEVEN

Captain Dragan Spasic laid the map of Yugoslavia on the table and wrote '*Potkovica*' ('The Horseshoe') on it with a black marker. 'Potkovica' was the secret code for the Serbian military operation against the Albanian population in Kosovo. He felt a pain all over his body and tried to focus on the details of the drawing on the map. He still had the taste of *Slivovica* in his mouth and felt his head heavy, because of heavy drinking from the previous night.

His hands shook a little as he opened the drawer and took out a file with the same name "*Potkovica*" written on it and started to read the instructions from the Ministry of Interior. After a few minutes he closed it impatiently. He felt uncomfortable in his office as the chief of police of Gjakova city. His view darkened and he scratched himself—his skin was becoming so itchy. He got up from the armchair and looked at himself in the mirror. Deep in the retinas of his eyes he noticed two little yellow fires. He glanced at the bookshelf where an oil painting hung on the wall. The Slavic mythic figure of Dazhbog, the wolves' shepherd, stared back at him. That painting was a gift to him by Slavco Mijetic, a painter from Belgrade. Dragan leaned toward the painting and studied it carefully. Dazhbog was a messenger from God, and was depicted standing between two large reclining wolves.

I am not feeling good, since that day I hung it on the wall. You are not the messenger! I am Dazhbog myself, the shepherd of the wolves! I say that clearly and I am not drunk or tired. Your angry look keeps following me all over the office! Better to take it off the wall! What's the purpose of giving a Dazhbog painting as a gift to someone anyway?

Dragan Spasic turned to his table and seized a greeting card. He held it as if it were the most valuable thing in the world. The card depicted an original picture taken from his home village of Grncar, located in the municipality of Babushnica in Central Serbia. He placed the card back on the table and touched the epaulet on his shoulder. Since he was promoted to chief of police, Dragan Spasic had not been sleeping well. Even though this was an honour to be celebrated, he felt a heavy burden on his shoulders. It had always been like this, since that day when he had graduated from the Post Secondary Police School in Zagreb, and again between 1975 and 1980 when he had worked as a policeman at the Public Security Station SJB in Gjakova.

Dazhbog kept staring at him from the painting, and he felt his skin becoming itchy again. He scratched both forearms so hard with his nails that he scored tiny lines of blood on them. He licked the blood with the tip of his tongue and felt pleased.

Definitely I'm not feeling well, since I am doing these things to myself. Either I am experiencing a mental disorder or something alien is happening to my body. My nails have grown too long, so long I am scared of myself. I should cut them off. I've been too busy getting rid off these Albanians that I don't have time for my personal grooming any more. When was the last time I cut my nails? Probably a month ago?! Hmm!

Dragan studied the tips of his fingers and thought that his nails resembled those of wolves. They were very long and blackened and bent a little. Even his hair was thicker and wild. He grew terrified and decided not to think about that any more. He had to take care of more important things than grooming himself. The diplomas that hung on the wall put him in a good mood again, but Dazhbog kept staring at him with mistrust from the frame on the wall.

It's just a painting. Why do I have to pay so much attention to it and treat it as a real human being?! He is not a man who breathes; it's just a big monster that causes changes in me. Probably these long nails belong to Dazhbog. Am I him, or is he me?! God damn it! I better focus on the trouble in my city.

In a few minutes he had to join a meeting with military personnel and volunteer groups who supported action against the Albanians. He rubbed his temples with stubby fingers. He drew out a book from the shelf, *The Expulsion of the Albanians,* written by Vaso Cubrilovic in 1937, and flipped through the pages. He was always fascinated by the arguments of Professor Cubrilovic on the expulsion of Albanians. Dragan had reread that book several times, whenever he felt bored. Vaso Cubrilovic was his spiritual leader and Dragan had studied his works in detail since he was a student. One of the most interesting facts that addicted him to Cubrilovic's thesis was the biography of the professor. In his youth, Cubrilovic took part in the assassination of Franz Ferdinand, the Archduke of Austro-Hungarian Empire, and his wife Sophie on June 28, 1914. The death of Ferdinand triggered the beginning of the First World War.

"Serbia began to slice off pieces of this Albanian wedge as early as the first uprising by expelling the northernmost Albanian settlers from Jagodina. Thanks to the wide-ranging national plans of Jovan Ristic, Serbia sliced off another piece of this wedge with the annexation of Toplica and Kosanica. At that time, the regions between Jastrebac and southern Morava were radically cleared of Albanians," he read out loud.

My dear professor didn't have to mention that these lands belonged to the Albanians. It's the same as proving that we the Serbs are the newcomers here. That we are guilty before the court. He didn't have to show the world the real northern border of the Albanians. However, I totally agree with him that "Serbia has to use brutal force against the Albanians."

He replaced the book on the bookshelf and sat in his armchair. Dazhbog stared at him from the frame. Dragan circled the word "Potkovica" on the map with a pencil and added a few arrows, which pointed toward the border of Albania and Macedonia. The plan for the expulsion of the Albanians from Kosovo wasn't a secret anymore. The Bulgarian Intelligence Agency had revealed the plan to the German Intelligence Agency. Foreign Minister of Germany Joshka Fisher had made it public at NATO headquarters in Brussels.

If we really want to kick the Albanians out, we have to do it right now, otherwise it will be too late. Many of them are getting the hell out of here, on tractors, dump trucks, carts, even on foot, and are going straight to Albania or Macedonia. The whole Albanian population of Prishtina got on a train and cleared out. How am I going to kill them if everyone leaves? I've got to do something to stop them from escaping. It's easier to shoot them right at the door. We have to go door to door and calm them down; we have to cool them down and make them believe that nothing is going to happen if they decide to stay in their homes. Then, if we reach that goal, we will attack them at their weakest point: we will shoot their children and women first.

Did Dazhbog wink at him in approval?! Or was it just an illusion? Or was he dreaming with his eyes wide open?! Dragan Spasic couldn't stand that painting. He rubbed his beard thoughtfully and took out an album of photographs from a drawer. He picked one of them and looked at it with pride. Standing beside him in the photograph was Zjelko Raznatovic Arkan, the chief of the White Tigers paramilitary group. A huge Serbian flag hung in the background as Arkan posed for the camera, holding a toy baby tiger in his left hand and a Kalashnikov automatic gun in his right. Behind him, a squadron of White Tigers were hailing the sky with a spray of bullets.

Someone knocked on the door as he lit a Cuban cigar and inhaled impatiently.

"Captain Spasic! The guests are waiting for you outside." His blonde secretary stuck her head around the door, which was halfway open.

Vera Ivanovic was shocked at Spasic's filthy look, but pretended that she didn't notice it. Her eyebrows darted up, then she pulled the door shut behind her in silence.

"I'll be there in a few seconds," said the captain, and squeezed the Cuban cigar on the ashtray. He put his blue jacket on and fixed the police hat on his head and looked at himself in the mirror. He left the office and descended the marble stairs, his long black boots pounding the floor in an ominous rhythm. The front door of the police station was all glass, so he could see through to the parking lot where a dozen paramilitary groups and civilians stood in line beside the policemen of his station. There were six squadrons and all of them had semi-automatic weapons slung on their shoulders. Captain Spasic saluted them and walked in front of the squadrons appreciatively. Most of the volunteer fighters were under the age of forty. Some of them wore camouflage uniforms and others wore military uniforms. Very few wore civilian clothes. Less than half of the fighters carried Zastava pistols hanging from their belts. There were five squadrons in total and every one of them was presenting their own volunteer group at the meeting with the chief of the local police. Most of their names were known to him.

He approached the commander of the first squadron, Blago Stojkovic, a childhood friend. Their group was called "Sakali" ("The Jackals"). Blago had cut his mustache really short, similar to Hitler's. Before he came to serve in Kosovo, Dragan had been together with Blago in Bosnia, where they served on the front line against the Bosnian Muslims and Croats. He recalled them having lunch inside the entrenchment when bombs flew over their heads, but they didn't leave. They finished their meal and went back to fight.

Dragan continued his walk, saluting the squadrons with respect and appreciation. Lubomir Stoinic commanded the second squadron. He was born in Northern Mitrovica. His squadron held members of the paramilitary group "Skorpions," which had taken responsibility for blowing up several Albanian homes in Southern Mitrovica. Seven kids, five women, and two elders were killed by the explosives thrown by Lubomir and his comrades.

Ratko Sejsel was the chief of "the Black Hand." He came from Belgrade. Ratko served the first line of duty in Srebrenica, Bosnia, where seven thousand Bosnian Muslims, mostly women and children, were slaughtered by the Serbian regular forces and paramilitary groups. A bullet wounded him in the right eye as he was taking part in an attack against the civilian population in Bosnia. Since then he had to cover the eye with a black leather patch tied around his head. Ratko didn't like to talk too much and always stayed aloof from the others. When someone wanted to ask him a question, he answered with very few words, using mostly just "yes" or "no."

The fourth commander wasn't really a guest. Miroslav Kapetanovic was still a member of the police force, who joined with other volunteer groups as many times as they had to organize the invasions against the Albanians.

Captain Spasic licked his dry lips with the tip of his tongue and looked at them triumphantly.

"Soldiers of Serbia!" he shouted to those assembled. "I called all of you here on this historic day to let you know that our Operation 'Potkovica' is underway and has reached a decisive phase. We must attack the enemy in his weakest point and not let him escape. We have to fight them until the last drop of blood is shed. We should not exclude anybody if we have even the slightest doubt that one of their family members has connections with the terrorist KLA. Every single one of them might be either a military or police target. This will be a joint operation, and the police force will be backed up either by the army or volunteer groups."

Captain Spasic paused for a moment, but that was enough for the militants to erupt in frenetic applause.

"Urraah, may God bless Serbia!"

Captain Spasic came closer and saluted them by raising three fingers in the air, reminding them of the Trinity. "*Nema krsta bez tri prsta.*" ("There is no cross without three fingers.")

"Do you know what these three fingers in the air mean? One finger is dedicated to St Sava, the other finger is for Karagjorgje, and the third finger for Njegosh. There is no Serbia without Kosovo. What do I mean that 'all Albanians might be legitimate targets?' I mean we should not have any mercy. If we have even a little mercy, then we might be in very big trouble!"

"There is no mercy! Urraah!" one of the commanders shouted, as the rest joined him in chorus. Spasic felt relieved. A volunteer waved a huge Serbian flag above his head. Captain Spasic took the binoculars from Miroslav's hand and focused his gaze on the main road. The convoy of refugees was slowly approaching the police roadblock. They all looked exhausted. Already covered by the dust of oblivion, they had no clue what surprise awaited them.

"There is just one little problem!" said Dragan, gazing back at those assembled before him. "As you can see, the *Shiptari* are leaving *en masse*. We have to clean them up from the whole stretch alongside the border with Albania. In the meantime, we have to question or eliminate Albanian males who are leaving along with their families. Our Ministry of Interior has info that most of the Albanian males are joining KLA ranks as soon as they cross the border. The best way to deal with this is to separate them from their families and shoot them on the spot. There is no time left to imprison them or transport them somewhere else. All suspicious elements have to be executed on the scene. I stress once again that this operation we cannot conduct alone. The army, the police, the paramilitary groups should coordinate their actions to complete the operation successfully. Every single one of you is welcome: "The Scorpions, "Legija," "Black Hand," "The White Tigers," "The Chetniks," "The Jackals," members of the special units—even prisoners who love their country and want to be side by side with their army."

"Yes, Captain!" Miroslav Kapetanovic said. "We are going to search for the Albanian terrorists even in the rat's hole."

"Every single bomb that NATO is throwing on us will be repaid by a hundred Albanians," said Spasic firmly, stressing every word.

"Sir! Yes, sir!" all the squadrons shouted in one loud voice.

"All right, then! Go back to your units and keep up the good work that you already started." The captain concluded and saluted them again with the three finger sign.

He turned back to the office and felt quite relieved as Dazhbog looked at him from the wall. Standing one inch away from the painting, Dragan stared back at Dazhbog with defiance.

"I am Dazhbog from now on, and not you in the painting. Stay where you are, in my body, in my heart and my soul! You are very welcome!" he murmured and grabbed a bottle of *Slivovica* from the bookshelf.

EIGHT

It was almost four AM when five Serbian policemen broke down the basement door. Valbona Bllaca stood aside and opened her arms instinctively as if trying to hide all four of her children behind her. The three girls and the boy crouched toward her. Valbona recognized one of the officers. He was their neighbour, who lived just a few doors away from their home.

"That's Nenad's father," Ermal said softly, recognizing the policeman's short mustache and big nose. Valbona squeezed Ermal's hand a little, signaling him not to speak. A sudden movement could cost them their lives. She had heard a lot of stories about Albanians being shot or stabbed on the slightest pretext.

"Ku janë ushtarët e UÇK-së?" ("Where are the KLA soldiers?") Dragan Spasic asked Valbona in Albanian.

"Nuk e di. Këtu jemi vetëm gra dhe fëmijë!" ("I don't know! We are just children and women here!") she responded in Albanian.

"Everybody move! Get out now!" Dragan yelled at them.

Shaking, Valbona struggled to understand how it was possible that the police discovered them in that dungeon basement. She realized then why the families of the Serbian police were wedged between Albanian homes in the neighbourhood of Qerim. The reason was as clear as day: the Serbs wanted to keep an eye on the Albanian population. It was too little too late to come to that conclusion. The Albanians were caged in like animals.

"Keep moving," he ordered.

Valbona lifted her youngest daughter in her arms and stepped outside. Hana pulled her brother and sister by the hand. One by one, the women and children emerged from the basement. The women's faces changed colour from white to the yellow wax of terror. The dark sky was filled with stars. A waning moon seemed to bid them a final farewell. Fear made them shake even more than the cold.

The policemen looked very nervous as they pushed the Albanian women and children along with their guns. They herded them to the nearest house beside the pool. When they arrived there, Florija, the youngest daughter of Arben, ran ahead of the group and pulled at the door handle, but she couldn't open it. Dragan pulled a revolver from his holster and fired a single shot at the bolt. Florija screamed in fright and ran to her mother. The door cracked open.

Dragan waved the revolver in his hand and yelled, "Get inside one by one!"

Three policemen divided them in two small groups and stood in the middle of the living room, pointing their guns at them. Dragan stood at the exit. Valbona looked in vain for her husband. She felt her whole body shiver and feared that he might have been killed.

The policemen yelled at them to kneel down. There were twenty-one people inside, from a two-year-old to Hekuran, a handicapped man of about sixty. Their faces were white with terror. The silence of death hung over their heads. They were quiet, gripped by the fear that the end had come.

Florija rose unexpectedly and put a pot on the stove to make some tea. Valbona couldn't understand why she wanted to make tea at that moment. Dragan pointed the revolver straight at her and shot her in the chest. Her mother ran wailing to her and she too was hit by bullets. The children started to scream. The three policemen opened fire at them all at once. Valbona felt something wet under her neck. She put out her hand and saw the tips of her fingers wet with blood. She was hit by a spray of bullets.

As Valbona fell, she looked at her son instinctively. A bullet had wounded him. Dreading that he was going to be killed before her eyes, Valbona covered him with her own body to protect him as she fell.

Ermal read deep in her eyes. She was saying to him: *I love you, son! I want you to live!*

Valbona didn't move. It wasn't just Ermal who was covered by her body. The youngest sister Diona also lay under her as well. She was crying loudly. As the policemen kept shooting at them, Ermal just gave up on her for the moment and played dead.

He lost all sense of time. The seconds felt like minutes and the minutes felt like hours. He saw one of the policemen checking the bodies one by one. A policeman stood over Ermal and fired. Ermal felt a bullet comb through his hair. He turned his head and held his breath. He heard the policeman's steps on the wooden floor. He sighed deeply and breathed slowly. But smoke was filling the room.

Ermal coughed hard and looked around in panic. The policemen weren't there. He pushed his mother's body aside and got to his feet. Tongues of fire were licking at the walls. The policemen had set the house on fire!

Hana and Trëndelina showed no signs of life. Were they dead? He touched Trëndelina, but she didn't react. Her eyes were half open, focused on the ceiling. Ermal felt his heart pounding. He crept over to Hana and noticed that she moved a little. She handed him a handkerchief, so he could cover his nose. The smoke grew thicker and heavier. When he turned his head towards her again, she'd closed her eyes and stopped moving. Ermal didn't want to believe that she had just taken her last breath. He called her back from where she was going. "Hana, Hana! It's me, Ermal!"

Hana couldn't hear him. She was dead.

As he was about to leave, he heard a weak sound. Diona was still moaning under Valbona's body. Their mother had saved just two of her children. Ermal tried to pull Diona out, but his arm was not moving. He felt searing pain through the bone. His arm was bleeding. He guessed that he had caught a bullet in his arm. He realized that he had to leave right away if he wanted to stay alive. That was the last hope his mother had conveyed to him with her eyes as she fell.

Ermal ran as fast as he could. He looked around and noticed a window. He grabbed a chair, moved it closer to the wall and climbed up on it. He struggled to see through the blinds. Two policemen were drinking beer and smoking cigars. What if they returned? What would happen next? He had to play dead again. He had to stay that way, but the smoke was becoming denser. He went to the salon in order to escape from being suffocated and lay there, pretending to be dead. He didn't move for a few more minutes, but the cloud of smoke covered everything, making it difficult to breathe. He looked out the window and noticed that the two policemen were not there anymore.

Ermal jumped into the backyard only to face a two-meter-high wall. He dragged three empty crates on top of each other and was able to climb it. He fell into the yard of the house next door and frantically searched around. There was nobody there. It seemed that everyone had gone somewhere to escape the militants. He slowly went inside and approached a window that looked out in the direction of the officers, without moving the curtain. He was trembling with fear and pain. His left arm was in excruciating pain and bleeding a lot. He felt weak and almost fainted. His lips were dry from thirst, and his throat was sore. He opened the fridge and found some milk and drank it in big gulps. His aunt's house was only two doors away, but Ermal did not dare to go near it after hearing the army trucks passing down the road. He hid under a bed and waited until it was quiet.

The main door was open, but he did not dare leave. He was running out of courage and hope. He had to do something to stop the bleeding. He ripped up his T-shirt and wrapped it around the wound. It seemed to stop the bleeding.

Finally, Ermal crawled out and left the house. He jumped over a wall and found himself in another house, which had also been abandoned. The whole neighbourhood must be deserted, he thought. He wondered where all the people had gone. He stayed a long while without moving from the spot where he lay in the yard. He stayed until dawn, when he heard the first roosters crowing.

Ermal looked out toward the woods. If he entered the forest, then he could hope to stay alive. He opened the fridge in another abandoned house and stole some bread and cheese. He took a water bottle and put everything in a bag. He tied another T-shirt around his left arm and looked out into the backyard. He didn't see anybody.

His arm continued to bleed, and for a moment he thought he would die. His view was darkening. He climbed the last wall and finally fell right into the backyard of his Aunt Fatima's house. Had they also gone away? He wondered what to do next.

As he was losing hope, Aunt Fatima came out of the cellar. Ermal was sitting in the stairwell, supporting his head against the wall, only half-conscious.

* * * *

The sky became bright and the leaves were a bright red colour. I noticed someone coming up to me with light steps. I lifted my head and saw the silhouette of a tall woman dressed in red. She had long black hair that was waving in the morning breeze. Her blue eyes were filled with a magical light. I was shaking from head to toe. Was I dreaming or was I delirious? I lifted my hands to touch her, but the woman smiled and told me not to move.

"Mami, how is this possible?" I asked the silhouette, but the silhouette didn't speak. She just gave me a light kiss on the forehead.

"I thought you were dead," I whispered, as my breath became heavier.

"I was worried, so I came back to see you," the woman said. She was wrapped in a white sheet of mist. She came closer and hugged me. I was scared. I didn't believe in ghosts, in dreams either, but she was my Mami, standing in front of me like nothing was wrong.

"I saw what happened down here," she said, "I saw everything. Then I met all the new ghosts who came up to where I am. It's already overcrowded up there."

I gulped. A hundred questions came into my mind.

"So, you met all of them?" I asked and my spine was shuddering.

"Yes, all of them!"

"Did you see Trendy?"

"I saw Trendy!"

I was shocked. That meant that Trëndelina was dead.

"Did you see Grandma?" I asked her.

"Yes, Grandma too!" the woman said.

"Diona?"

"I met every single one: your grandma, grandfather and your aunt," my mother said.

I couldn't hold back my tears. That meant that all of them had been killed.

"I guess I am the only survivor. I am the only one who is still breathing!"

"Yes, you are the only one left alive."

Big teardrops fell from her eyes. I felt my heart pounding really hard.

"What about Balash?" I asked.

Balash was our dog, a big hairy dog that had lived with us for more than ten years. I missed him so much already. I missed his barking in front of the house. He was our guard who kept us awake and aware of the Serbian patrols passing by, hunting the Albanians down.

"Balash probably escaped to the forest," my mother said, and vanished before my eyes.

* * * *

Ermal saw her silhouette in his sleep. Aunt Fatima disappeared for a moment, and after a few minutes she came back and slapped him on the face. He shook his head and woke up. He looked straight into her eyes.

"Where's your *Mami*? Where are your sisters?" she asked him. Her eyes were wide open, filled with terror.

He gathered all his strength to speak to her. "Everyone's been killed!"

Aunt Fatima hugged him and held him tight for a few seconds. She didn't want to believe what she had heard.

"It's not true, not true," she muttered. "You've seen a bad dream. Wake up."

She shook his shoulders slightly as if to awaken him from sleep. Then she noticed that her hand was covered with blood. "Oh, my God! You're wounded! Let's get you inside!"

Right then Grandfather Hamza and Adem came outside. Adem ran to his son and lifted him into his arms. He squeezed Ermal tightly and wept in silence. Was that the second time he was seeing his Babi cry? Adem trembled as if the earth was shaking under his feet.

"The Serbian police killed all of them," the boy said, and the whole world closed around him. The sky turned dark and he didn't know where he was.

* * * *

I was running through the woods of Pashtrik's Mountain. My feet were dripping with blood. My breath was becoming heavier and my wounded arm was hurting beyond the limits of endurance. I heard the sound of water close to the footpath. I followed the stream and found a little well filled with clear water. I put my dry lips to the spring water and drank as much as I could. I lay on my back on the ground, which was wet because of the night dew, and closed my eyes so I could forget everything I went through that day. I had no idea how long I stayed that way.

Someone was licking my face. I squeezed my fists and opened my eyes. Balash was right beside me. He quivered and kept licking me with his thin, long tongue. I could swear I saw tears in his eyes. I hugged him like never before. He kept me warm with his body all night long. I looked around and realized that I had been asleep right beside a fallen oak tree, not far from a roadblock built right in the middle of the highway by the White Tigers.

Fear made my spine quiver. I closed my eyes immediately to play dead. I heard someone talking in Serbian, but couldn't understand anything. I knew very little Serbian.

I better not move at all and pretend I am dead, otherwise they will finish me for good, I thought – but Balash had other ideas. He bit into my clothes and dragged at me in order to get me to run. I sighed and got up and ran as fast as I could. Balash chased after me with joy, since I was obeying his orders. I heard more shotguns firing and women and children screaming not far from where I was. I didn't want to believe that the Serbs were attacking the refugee line on the main road.

In a matter of minutes, I lost consciousness. I felt blood on my face and something very strong drilling deep in my right arm.

A hand fell on my left shoulder. The hand didn't move any longer and I realized that it belonged to a dead woman. I opened one eye and saw myself surrounded by dozens of dead women.

A truck stopped not far from where I was and a group of soldiers got on it. Two soldiers grabbed me by my legs and arms and threw me on the roadside. In a matter of seconds, I felt other bodies falling on top of me. I tried to lift my right hand in order to make some space for breathing, but remembered that I had to stay still. I heard footsteps going in the opposite direction and the sound of shotgun fire nearby.

NINE

The truck stopped right in front of the ruins of the Bllaca home, from which a cloud of smoke was still spewing out. Blago Stojkovic, the head of the "Jackals," jumped down from the cabin and covered his nose with the palm of his hand. The whole area stank with the stench of burned bodies. He coughed and vomited sideways, as he noticed a handful of Roma people who were taking the dead out of the ruins, surrounded by a cordon of policemen. It was three o'clock in the morning and the whole operation for hiding the dead bodies was being achieved under torchlight. Blago Stojkovic looked up at the sky to see if there was a NATO plane flying overhead. The torchlights were used very sparingly and were too faint to be noticed by the NATO planes. His fear eased, and he began to feel more comfortable. As he walked to the back of the truck to open the doors, his cellphone rang.

"Hello, Captain? Yes, yes! We'll collect every single bone! As you say, sir! We will check the attics, the basements, the backyards, everywhere. We are not going to leave even a single hole without checking it. We are ready for everything that Serbia will ask us to do! Thank you, Captain!"

Blago Stojkovic shut off the cellphone and frowned. The other paramilitary members around him didn't dare to ask him what the captain said, and stepped back a little frightened instead. Blago had the nickname "Shumadija," but "the Jackals" simply called him "boss" most of the time. They all wore gold uniforms, to resemble golden jackals. Their death squad was one of the most well known in Yugoslavia and were part of the 177th division of the Yugoslav army. Their headquarters was located in Peja city ("Pec" in Serbian), but they had come to Gjakova city to join the military campaign against the Albanian civilians.

The Jackals stepped back a little, waiting around the truck until Roma workers were done removing the remains of the dead. There were ten Jackals altogether. Three of them were smoking. Two, who were drinking *Slivovica*, stopped for a second and covered their noses with handkerchiefs. The oldest of the jackals, a forty-five-year-old man of average height, grabbed another can of beer from the case and handed it over to the commander. He limped along on a wooden leg. He'd lost his left foot stepping on a mine in the Bosnian war. His name was Nemanja Djuric, but his nickname was "the handicap." He breathed heavily and sounded like he was drunk. He licked his lips and blew his nose sideways.

"What's new, Shumadija?" he asked the commander, standing awkwardly.

Blago liked it when he called him "Shumadija." The militants were calling him "Daddy" as well, since he was the oldest. "Daddy" was a name he got from the war in Bosnia. All of them were called "The Golden Jackals," a name he chose himself for his own group. The jackal, this proud animal, was mentioned fourteen times in the Bible. Fourteen times. Feeling proud and exerting his authority, Blago grabbed the can from the hand of the youngest of the Sakali group and threw it away. Some discipline was needed to show who they were, for God's sake. They were not just a bunch of big heavy drinkers, they were soldiers as well.

"I just got a phone call from the captain," said Blago, his voice shivering with anxiety and impatience. Trying to gain their full attention, he whistled, putting two fingers into his mouth. The Jackals who were drinking set their drinks aside and stood up. The smokers threw their cigarette butts away and rushed to stand in front of the commander. The volunteers who were taking a break joined their friends, waiting in silence.

"As I said, I just spoke to Captain Spasic on the phone. He reminded me of our job once again: we have to collect all the dead bodies around here. Nothing has to escape our eyes. The captain gave us an order that the whole operational area has to be under surveillance. We have to make them disappear. No bodies, no witnesses to testify against us. I'll drive the truck straight to Serbia," he said, glancing at the dead that were being loaded on to the truck.

"There are a lot of them. We might need two more trucks," Nemanja Djuric said.

"I know! Let's fill this up first," Blago said. "There are hundreds of them locked in their homes, in the basements, even under the roofs." He paused and gazed at them as if they were kids, kids who knew nothing about the tactics of ethnic cleansing. His tall, well-built body matched his imperious gaze and commanded the respect of the death squad volunteers.

Unconvinced that his drunken fighters understood what he meant, Blago grabbed the youngest volunteer by his shoulders and squeezed him tight, like he was waking him up from a deep sleep.

"Do you really know what you have to do?" he yelled at him.

"Yes, sir! One thousand per cent!" the volunteer yelled back at him with zeal.

"You are the best men I have! Let's start without losing a minute!"

"A question for you, sir," asked another volunteer, a man around forty who looked sober. He also looked frightened.

"Sure, go ahead!" Blago encouraged him.

"What should we do if an Albanian man appears in front of us holding a gun?"

He stepped toward him, patted him on the shoulder and looked triumphantly at the rest of the fighters. He had to disperse the clouds of doubt and build self-confidence in these death squads. The whole group of Sakali was waiting for his answer.

"The short answer is: we kick his ass! We shoot him and cut his skull into one thousand little pieces! Did all of you guys get that?" he shouted at them fiercely.

"Sir, yes, sir!" the chorus of fighters shouted enthusiastically. Their shouts rang out. In a matter of seconds, there was much noise as bullets hailed overhead in response to the speech of Blago Stojkovic. The men started to sing "March on the Drina," a song written by Stanislav Binicki:

"To battle, go forth, you heroes,
Go on and don't regret your lives
May Cer see the front, may Cer hear the battle
And river Drina glory, courage
And heroic hand of father and son!

Sing, sing, Drina - of cold water,
Remember, and tell of the ones that fell,
Remember the brave front,
Which full of fire, mighty force
Expelled the foreigner from our dear river!

Sing, sing, Drina, tell the generations,
How we bravely fought,
The front sang, the battle was fought
Near cold water
Blood was flowing,
Blood was streaming
By Drina for freedom!"

TEN

When Ermal Bllaca woke up, he found himself in a bed with Grandfather Hamza, Aunt Fatima and Babi Adem sitting beside him. His arm was wrapped up in bandages. Aunt Fatima put some vinegar on a rag and placed it on his forehead. He had a high fever.

Adem kissed his son on the cheek.

"You will go with Aunt Fatima to Albania," Adem said.

Ermal knew Babi couldn't come with him. Most of the male Albanians were separated from their families and killed at once by Serbian army and police.

"What about you?" Ermal asked.

"I'll go from house to house to the woods, until I reach the mountain. I'll meet you in Albania," Adem said.

"Babi, am I going to see you again?"

"Yes, son! You have my word on this," Adem said and turned his back. Ermal saw him leave and felt a chill in his heart. What if it was their last meeting? He tried to get up on his elbows in bed and call him to stop, but his arm could not support his weight. He fell back unconscious.

Ermal woke again in his aunt's house, but this time he was completely alone. His aunt came into the room.

"Wake up! Child, wake up!" It was the sweet voice of Aunt Fatima. Her eyes were filled with tears. He vaguely saw her, and suddenly the clouds of tears left her eyes.

Ermal used to have a lot of fun at his aunt's house. His aunt was home alone most of the time. Her husband was killed by the Serbs ten years ago and she never got married again. Aunt Fatima treated him as her own son. Her house became his second home after spending so many weekends with his aunt and Grandfather Hamza. Ermal loved his aunt so much. Once he expressed that to his mother and she got mad at him. She felt jealous or something, but then quickly cooled down. Aunt Fatima was her sister anyway and she loved her too.

Aunt Fatima helped him put on a new shirt and changed the

bandage on his wounded arm. She tied his arm with another bandage which she looped around his neck.

"Get up slowly, love! We are going to Albania," said Aunt Fatima.

Ermal put his right hand on her shoulder to steady himself as he got up. Grandfather Hamza had started his old field tractor in the front yard. It was the first time that Ermal would be going to Albania, a country he had heard so many beautiful stories about.

He had mixed feelings about the journey and the pain from the bullet in his arm was still bad. They took the main street and there he saw that the road was full of Albanians fleeing from their homes. Most of them were women and children. He wondered where the male Albanians had gone. The convoy of refugees was becoming too long. Gjakova had become a ghost town. Grandfather Hamza was driving his yellow Yugo field tractor so slow, only ten miles per hour, and they were shivering from the cold. Aunt Fatima covered the boy with blankets up to his neck. Ermal closed his eyes and tried to nap, but the bullet in his arm hurt too much. It felt as though it was sliding in deeper and deeper.

His curiosity of what had happened to the male Albanians was soon satisfied. They reached a roadblock at the entrance of Meja village. The policemen stopped the convoy and separated some of the male members from their families. A policeman ordered a forty-year-old Albanian to hand his child over to the wife, then drew him aside as the other family members objected. The Serbian police let the rest go and told the man to stay on the side of the road, a few meters away. Ermal lifted his head from under the blanket and noticed that on the barren field there were around fifty men of different ages, ranging from sixteen to seventy years old. The men were ordered to kneel down, with their hands tied and crossed behind their backs. In a matter of seconds, a squadron of the Serbian military stood in a line in front of them and sprayed them with bullets.

Ermal had never seen such a scene in his entire life. The shooting from a few meters away wasn't enough! One of the soldiers approached the fallen men and shot them in the head with a pistol, making sure that none of them escaped alive.

Aunt Fatima screamed in horror and pushed her nephew to sit back on the seat immediately, covering his eyes with her hand. Grandfather Hamza pressed the gas pedal and the old tractor lumbered slowly along the road, carrying its load of grief.

Ermal removed his aunt's hand to see what was going on. He stared at the Serbian militants and gulped in fear. A few meters away from the spot where the Albanian men were killed, there was a little hill of piled bodies, a human hill streaming with blood. He had forgotten the pain that the wound was causing to his arm and was looking at the face of an Albanian man on the pile of bodies who was still breathing and had his eyes open. The man was waving at the convoy for help. He was trying to get out of the big pile of dead bodies, but he couldn't since the pile was way too heavy and held him under.

Ermal kept staring at the dying man and didn't notice the second roadblock, which was set up a few yards ahead by the Serbian militants.

A masked militant with a Kalashnikov gun slung over his shoulder ordered the tractor to stop. Grandfather Hamza shut the engine off and sat frozen behind the wheel. The militant got on the tractor and looked at the passengers inside carefully. His eyes rested on Ermal, whose wounded arm was seeping blood. The militant's face darkened as he pulled the blanket to have a better look at the boy. He came closer to the back seat, where Ermal was sitting.

"What happened to your arm?" he asked Ermal.

Aunt Fatima struggled to find the right answer. One little mistake could be disastrous. "He was playing soccer and broke his arm," she said in halting breaths.

"Take the bandage off! I want to see the wound!" he insisted.

Aunt Fatima shook from head to toe. She put a hand in her purse and pulled out a wad of new euro banknotes. There were twenty euro bills, five hundred all together, nicely tied and saved for bad days. That money was the life savings that one of her sons brought with him when he came to Kosovo from Germany. She handed the banknotes to the militant.

"Please, leave him alone!" she begged with trembling lips. "He is just a ten-year-old kid and I'm afraid he will die on my hands. He has so much pain and we cannot afford to lose time, but take him straight to the hospital."

The Serbian militant softened a little when he saw the bundle of euro banknotes. He grabbed the money and stuck it deep into his pocket. He jumped off the tractor and waved at Grandfather Hamza to drive forward.

"Come on; get the hell out of here!" he said sharply. Grandfather Hamza started the engine and the old tractor lurched forward. Aunt Fatima closed her eyes in relief.

Ermal got up halfway from his seat and followed the militant with his eyes, not believing that they were already safe. Aunt Fatima pressed gently but firmly on his healthy shoulder, pushing him back into his seat. She winked at him to be quiet then opened a little suitcase beside her and taking out a sleeping pill, handed it over to him.

"Swallow it! It will ease your pain," she whispered and let him drink some water from a plastic bottle. Ermal chewed the pill with his teeth, thinking it was candy, but in fact it was a Valium pill. Within a few minutes his eyelids became heavy. Soon he felt he was flying across the sky and then sinking in a fog of dreams.

ELEVEN

I saw myself again in white clouds with my mother standing by. Her eyes were shining with a divine light as she came toward me without even moving her feet. She hugged me and held me for a bit in her arms. I felt her warmth penetrating my body. Her face was white. I shivered.

"Mami, I missed you so much," I said, holding her in my arms.

"Don't let yourself down, son. Go down there and take the killers to prison," she said.

"Go down there? Where am I? What's this place up here?" I asked. But she didn't answer. I saw her dissolving slowly into air, and then there was nothing. I wondered if I had crossed the border between the two worlds and was actually in heaven.

It was completely dark when I became conscious. I pushed a woman's body away and breathed freely. I pushed another body in order to move my feet, but I couldn't. Then I saw Balash once again pulling me out from that hole. I clenched my teeth and looked around. I had been dumped into a mass grave with bodies piled up on top of each other. I shivered and almost screamed with terror. I was extremely frightened.

I crawled out of the hole by using both hands and pushing hard with my feet. I saw the Serbian military base not far from the mass grave. All of a sudden Trendy came into my mind. What exactly happened to her? Where was my grandma? I stopped and turned toward the mass grave. It was almost impossible for me to identify them. I crawled in, but stopped very close to it, not feeling brave enough to get in there and dig inside. I was able to look at one of them, an old man in his eighties. A bullet had gone right through his chest. The unknown man looked like he was smiling with his eyes half open, and his mustache was covered with blood. I gulped and fell backward. There was no way I could get back in there. I stopped for a moment and looked around.

Then I saw Balash lying dead on the ground. At that point, I didn't have any more tears.

I have to stay away from the highway and disappear in the

woods if I want to survive, I thought, looking into the darkness.

* * * *

When Ermal woke up, he saw himself still lying on the back seat of the field tractor. He didn't have any idea how long they had been traveling. Hundreds of people were joining the convoy of refugees, all struggling to escape to Albania. Ermal tried to count them, but there were thousands. It seemed that almost all the Albanians were running for their lives. Many questions came into his tired mind, but there was no one who would give him answers. He wondered where his father was. Perhaps he was left behind, between the mountains, fighting for his life, or probably he was dead. Their dog Balash had disappeared somewhere, or had been killed.

The massive movement of people was making him sad. Was he going to be able to come back ever again to the old neighbourhood where he was born? If he was going to come back, when would it be? Of one thing he was sure: things were not going to be the same as before without Mami and his three sisters. He struggled with his thoughts, whenever he had a question, he tried to forget about it and move on. He looked at Aunt Fatima. She was one of the few relatives he had left. She was praying to God for no more Serbian militant encounters and no more roadblocks. She lifted her hands up to the sky and with her eyes staring in space, she mumbled: *"Oh dear Lord! It can't be worse than this. Please save this child at least. I pray to God that the Serbs will not stop us anymore on the road! We have to stay alive so we can tell the world what happened to us!"*

It seemed that her prayers were falling on deaf ears. After three hours another group of armed Serbs stopped them. They pointed guns at them. Ermal saw that they were smoking and drinking alcohol. Some of them looked nervous and jumped right away for money. Fatima took another bundle of euro banknotes out from her purse and handed it to them. The militants let them go, but their relief would not last long. Some of the Albanian men who didn't have any money were separated from their families and were taken to an unknown place.

It took them three days and three nights to come to the border with Albania. Before crossing it, the last Serbian patrol stopped the convoy and stripped all the refugees of their personal identification papers. All the license plates were taken off the vehicles and dumped on the side of the road. A policeman set the papers on fire in front of them. As soon as they passed the border at the crossing of Morine, the UNHCR workers ran toward them to help. A nurse from Kosovo took Ermal in his arms and carried him to a tent that was set up to give first aid. A crew of journalists and photographers surrounded them and eagerly asked questions, but Ermal couldn't speak because of his pain. His lips were dry and his body was so weak.

"Be strong, big boy! You survived for one reason: the world has to know what happened!" the nurse said to him and he started to untie the old crusted bandage around his wound. It felt like pieces of flesh were taken away with the old bandage. Ermal screamed and bit his lower lip. He almost fainted from the pain in his arm and he noticed that it was swollen. His view darkened and he burst into tears.

The journalists tried to get details from him of what had happened back there. What did the nurse say? *The world has to know what happened!* How could he describe what happened? Was there a magic power to describe in the right words what happened? Were there any words left?

* * * *

Their tent sat in the middle of a hundred others. A whole sea of people, mostly women and children, were sheltered temporarily in a field beside an old abandoned mine. Ermal searched the campground for his Babi, but didn't see him anywhere. An inner voice was telling him that his Babi was still alive.

If Babi reached the woods, then he must have made it. He would come out of the woods, walk through the rough pathways, which were still covered by a layer of ice and snow, and come to Albania.

He closed his eyes and prayed in silence for his father. Was Babi able to pass the border or was he killed by the Serbian army? Perhaps he got in touch with KLA soldiers and they helped him get out.

Within a few hours no vacant place remained. Thousands of expelled Kosovo Albanians had piled into the giant camp, which was built by the United Arab Emirates, the only non-member of NATO, who was trying to do their best to help the refugees. There was nothing missing at the UAE camp, they even set up a playground for the kids. Beyond that peaceful oasis, hundreds of people lined up in front of the trucks, which delivered bread. The refugees pushed each other in long lines, impatient to get their own loaf of bread. Wrinkled old men, sad women, tired kids with their eyes full of tears, waited for their turn. There were a few mobile bakery shops which were set up to work non-stop for twenty-four hours, but the delivery trucks were quickly emptied. The demand for bread was much higher than the amount produced on a daily basis. Bread was the main food on the table for an ordinary Albanian family. Without bread, the meal could not be eaten and the stomach would feel empty, no matter how tasty the dishes were. A twenty-year-old man was giving orders from the top of the truck, making sure that the refugees were moving forward, holding the line, and respecting each other.

Puma, a French military helicopter, arrived that afternoon in the northern town of Kukës. Ermal was airlifted the same day to the military hospital in Tirana. Aunt Fatima got on-board along with another three kids: another boy with a mortar injury, a girl whose foot was slashed by a grenade blast, and a baby with severe abdominal pain and high body temperature. There was no more room inside the helicopter as all the seats were occupied and the baby's mother panicked.

"I am not going to leave my child alone. Get him off," the young mother yelled, totally destroyed from fear and pain. Her name was Marigona and she was around twenty-five years old. The baby boy was probably a year old. Marigona's husband had been killed by the Serbs in front of her, and she arrived at the camp alone without any relatives.

"If we don't take your son to the hospital, he might not survive. He might die and you will remember that for the rest of your life. You will blame yourself that you didn't get him the medical help he needs," said the doctor.

The young woman didn't know what to do. She was still stretching her hands toward the helicopter and had shown so much pain on her face, as it looked like someone was pulling her heart out.

Aunt Fatima called out to her. "Marigona! I'll take care of your son. He can't wait even a minute. I give you my word that I'll take care of him. Hamza is going to give you a ride with his tractor to Tirana and both of you will join us at the military hospital. What do you say?"

"We will be in Tirana after seven hours' drive," Hamza assured her. "You will join your son as soon as we arrive there."

"All right then! Let's drive to the capital right now!" she said and stepped back from the helicopter, as the same doctor who warned her put the seatbelt around the bed where the little boy was lying. There was a double bed already set up inside the helicopter. Ermal stood on the lower bed, and waved at Grandfather with an uneasy smile on his face. The exit door shut and the pilot raised his thumb, giving the sign to take off. A huge cloud of dust circled the helicopter as it rose.

Ermal gazed out the little window and noticed Marigona getting on the tractor behind Grandfather Hamza in the driver's seat. He sighed and closed his eyes. It was time to forget everything just for a few seconds. It was the first time that he had ever got on a helicopter and he had a strange feeling as though he was living a dream.

What did the pilot say? Is he coming back to get more patients to the hospital?! Oh, thank God! Many people need immediate medical help!

The flight from the northern town of Kukës to Tirana didn't last more than an hour. It was a beautiful view from a hundred meters above. Ermal saw for the first time the light dusting of snow on the mountains. He kept lifting his head a little to catch every single detail of the flight, but the bullet wound on his arm reminded him to lie down. Unable to watch from the window, he simply closed his eyes and rested. When they arrived at the military hospital in Laprakë, on the outskirts of the capital Tirana, a team of nurses and doctors were waiting beside an ambulance, ready to rush the patients to the emergency room.

Ermal glanced around fearfully, looking for his aunt Fatima, but she seemed to be nowhere. He was totally alone in the emergency room with the hospital staff. He lifted his head from the stretcher and saw a handful of nurses and doctors with their masks on. For a moment he felt scared and wanted to run away, but the soft hands of a young nurse with blond hair pushed him gently back on the stretcher. He let his head fall on the pillow and looked to his right, at the entrance of the emergency room. There she was, Aunt Fatima, struggling to get his attention. She waved at him from behind the glass door. She was making sure that Ermal understood that "everything will be okay!" and there was nothing to worry about.

Ermal smiled a little and that was enough for Aunt Fatima to stop her waving.

In the room there were two monitors showing waves going up and down to the rhythm of his heart. A white mask was put under his nose and then he felt the effect of an anesthetic.

TWELVE

Ermal was completely wrapped up in bandages. He felt a hand brush his hair. He opened his eyes and noticed that his left arm was enclosed in a cast. He must be still dreaming, because he recognized his father. Adem had tears in his eyes and his lip trembled. He was sobbing quietly. Seeing him was the best moment after all the nightmares Ermal had been through.

"Try not to move," Adem said and turned his head sideways so his son would not see him crying. He wiped his tears and turned to look at him with reddened eyes. Ermal looked around for Aunt Fatima and Grandfather Hamza, but they were not there.

Perhaps Aunt Fatima went back to the camp to look after Grandfather. She would never leave me here alone. She probably changed her mind only when she saw Babi beside me.

"Babi, where is Aunt Fatima?"

"As soon as I arrived here, she left for Kukës. She is worried about your Grandfather, I guess! Why didn't he come with you by helicopter?" Adem asked his son.

"There wasn't enough room on the helicopter. It was just for emergency aid," the boy tried to explain through his exhaustion. Curiosity burned inside him. "Babi, how did you manage to escape?"

Adem sat on the corner of the bed, his voice shivering with mixed emotions.

"When I left..." His voice shook, his hands shook, even his lower lip trembled. Ermal had never seen his father cry that way before. Even when he turned his back to his son, Ermal noticed Babi's shoulders heaving with sobs. Adem wiped his tears with the back of his hand, drank a cup of water just to wet his throat, and then continued.

"As soon as the Serbian police and the militants surrounded the area, Arben and I jumped into the backyard of the next house. The policemen chased us for a while, but then Arben's father got their attention. He fought and died. The Serbs even used heavy weapons and anti-tank grenades on his house. After a while I didn't know where I was. I looked around for Arben and then realized he had been shot in the foot. I went along beside the fallen fence under cover of the smoke, carrying Arben, and finally reached another house a few meters away from the house which had collapsed in the hit. That house was almost untouched by the fire and the heavy artillery for one simple reason: it belonged to a Serb family who had left for Belgrade a long time ago. I hid Arben in the basement. Then I climbed into a very narrow space in the attic between the roof and the ceiling, and stayed there until no more gunshots were heard. I had the uneasy feeling that something very bad happened, so I couldn't wait any longer, but just jumped off the attic and came to Fatima's house, where I met you, and... learned about your mother and sisters." Here Adem broke off and sobbed uncontrollably. "After you left for Albania, I came back to the same house and pulled Arben from the basement, and both of us ran to the woods and met with KLA fighters who helped us cross the border. I was exhausted, but luckily didn't get hit by a bullet. Most of the time I was hurrying with Arben on my shoulder, not looking back at all. Every minute could cost our lives. I saw a tiny stream of water and knelt to wet my lips, which were dry with thirst. Right then a KLA soldier saw us and pointed his gun at us. Without their help, we would not have survived." Adem paused and stared at his son.

"Is that all?" Ermal asked him, eager to know all the details.

"We heard shots the whole time as we walked to the border. KLA fighters even came under a sudden attack of Serbian artillery and mortars, but none of us got killed or injured. It was just a small group of them, an advance unit of KLA behind the enemy lines. As soon as I crossed the border, I got a lift to Kukës city. I was sent to an UNHCR camp, where I had the time to think, and first thing I did was call our cousin in Switzerland to get international news on what was happening here. He recognized you on National Albanian TV. I guess you had some journalists as visitors, didn't you?"

Ermal nodded, eyes and ears directed to his father.

"We came by ambulance to the military hospital where you were. When we arrived at the post block in front of the hospital, I started to ask about you. The soldier let us in. As for Arben, he was taken straight to the surgery department. He is in a different room and will soon join us here. I left him there and found the Department of Heavy Trauma, where I saw you. First you were sleeping and I couldn't wait, but jumped on you and kissed your forehead. I still can't believe that I am seeing you!"

Adem ruffled Ermal's hair. His lower lip was still shivering with an inner sobbing. Father and son were facing a new reality. Adem couldn't keep the weeping under control any longer. He burst into tears and wept silently. After a few minutes he felt a little bit relieved. If he had kept the pain any longer inside his heart, his body might have fallen apart. *"At least I have my lovely son. Thank you, God! I'll have him beside me wherever I go!"*

"Now we are together again! I promise you, son, that I'll never leave you alone again. Who could think that the Serbian policemen would shoot innocent women and children? It's a terrible mistake that I didn't foresee what would happen! I was totally blind that I believed those beasts would have some human soul left in them. But thank God, you are alive."

His father was still shaking from pain and grief. He had such anger in his heart, but there was joy as well.

Adem got up from the corner of the bed where he was sitting and went to the window. The spirits of the dead were holding hands and had started to dance around the front yard of the hospital. He wiped his eyes, not believing what he saw! The ghosts disappeared instantly; it was just an illusion, nothing else.

Ermal fell asleep again and when he woke up, it was quite dark. The lights of Tirana capital looked like a huge sea of hope. The nurses came and went, paying visits every hour. After the surgery on his arm was done, Ermal was transferred to the pavilion of Neurology, Department of Heavy Trauma.

Adem kept his promise, never leaving Ermal alone, even during the medical procedures. The doctors and the nurses were kind, letting him follow all the medical treatment for his only living child. The only time he left Ermal alone was when he had to go to the market outside the hospital to buy fresh fruits and juices.

Soon the ten-year-old boy from Kosovo became a celebrity. The word spread that in their department a special guest was being treated. People started to visit his room, one after another donating fruits, jars of marmalade, conserves, and homemade sandwiches. But Ermal couldn't eat. His lips were dry because of a high body temperature and the wound on his arm still hurt a lot.

After a few days the doctors let him walk outside the room, into the main corridor of the hospital. It was there where a journalist from "Century 21" interviewed him. The journalist was surprised to hear how Serbian police killed his three little sisters and his mother. Adem was cautious and initially didn't want Ermal to be interviewed, still fearing for his son's life, but in the end he let his son speak. The war was now happening at a distance.

The interview with Ermal was published the next day. The first step was done: telling the world what happened. Adem could sense that Ermal had a burning desire to tell the story to the world himself, determined that everyone out there should know the ugly truth of what happened in Kosovo.

✽ ✽ ✽ ✽

The first days in the hospital passed quickly, but Ermal's mind was stuck in the past. He could hardly wait for Aunt Fatima and Grandfather Hamza to come and visit him. During the night, when everyone was sleeping, his mind travelled back, reliving the same frightening scene when twenty women and children were killed, his mother and three sisters included. He gasped in terror, sweating from head to toe. There was no more war outside. The war had got inside him instead. Ermal missed the whole world as he knew it, even Balash the dog, who used to live with them in their home. Even though he dreamt that Balash was killed by a sniper, he still had the feeling that Balash had escaped and was wandering around looking for him across the border.

As his father was looking sadly out the window late in the afternoon, he couldn't wait any longer. "Babi, do you have any idea when Aunt Fatima is coming back? Did she find Grandfather at the camp up north?" Ermal asked him.

"I spoke to a friend of mine on the phone. He has been at the camp for more than a week. There are thousands of people out there and it's too hard to find someone. Luckily he got in touch with some refugees from Gjakova and they told him that they saw Aunt Fatima and Grandfather Hamza in one of the tents. They will go back home as soon as Kosovo is liberated," said Adem and a little smile appeared on his sad face.

"Have you ever heard anything about Balash?!"

"We hope we will hear about Balash any time soon, probably when Aunt Fatima is back to the neighbourhood," Adem said and hugged his son.

THIRTEEN

It was the middle of April and spring was at its peak. The hospital had wide windows and a high ceiling so there was bright sunlight in Ermal's room. There were four beds in the ward, one still unoccupied. Adem was taking a nap in a chair, when a nurse brought Arben Morina into the room on a stretcher.

"Hey, look who is here!" Adem shouted and patted Arben on the shoulder.

"I found you, Adem Bllaca!" Arben tried to stretch his hand toward him, but felt very weak. His face was drawn in pain.

"Don't move! Let me help you!" He put his shoulder under Arben's arm as did the nurse from the other side of the stretcher and they helped him get on the vacant bed. The nurse bustled out of the room and Arben noticed Ermal in the other bed. He struggled to get up, but the wound on his left leg hurt a lot.

"Is that Ermal?" Arben asked. Ermal nodded with a grin on his face.

"You bet! He's the only one left from my family. God saved him, otherwise he would have been killed too."

"My two daughters are gone! My wife is gone! My father is gone! We have to do something to catch those killers." Arben closed his eyes to hide his despair. "Did you recognize anybody?" he asked Ermal.

"Yes! I know one of them! But there were five policemen altogether who shot at us."

"One is good enough to start hunting for the killers. What was his name?!"

"Dragan Spasic, our neighbour! He lives a few doors away from our home!"

"Oh, yes! I know him! How did he get such hatred for his neighbours? We never had problems with him. How do you know that it was really him?"

"I noticed his eyes, which were blue! I recognized the tattoo on his right arm, a tiger."

"Are you sure it was him?"

"Yes! I used to play soccer with his son, Nenad, in the soccer field beside the school, and Dragan came a couple of times and yelled at his son not to play with Albanians."

"What about the others, did you recognize them?"

"No."

"Don't worry. We'll find them!" said Arben. Several minutes passed and no one talked. The ghosts of his two daughters, his wife and his father were saying something, that only he could hear. Then he cried out, "Adem, we made a big mistake! We should have stayed with them and died altogether. Why do we still live?"

"Probably for a reason." Adem sighed deeply. "Dragan Spasic works at the police station in Gjakova. My guess is that all of them worked at the same station. We have to find the other four. There is no animal out there who can do this. If we call these criminals 'beasts' that would be an insult to the beasts."

"Five criminals who have to be captured and taken to court! My question is: who is going to capture them? Us?" Arben shook his head in disbelief. "And they are not just five! It might be a whole battalion who have blood on their hands. It's not just a matter of two or five families."

"We have to be patient! Kosovo will become a state and our government will seek justice!"

"That's just a dream!" said Arben. "Under the Serbian constitution, every citizen of Serbia is protected from extradition and it forbids the delivering of its citizens to foreign countries even in cases when sentences have been passed or the person is wanted by Interpol. If Kosovo becomes free after NATO's bombing, I will come back to town, to the same neighbourhood. I have to think big, and not just for you and myself. We have to seek justice for all the victims!"

"How you are going to do that? Is it going to be just you?"

"No way!" said Arben. "There will be plenty of people who want to seek revenge and justice. First I'll open an office. Second we will create some ads. It's going to be a volunteer job."

Adem leaned forward. "What job?"

"Tracking down these criminals wherever they are and giving the information to police, Interpol and, if this doesn't work, publish their names in the local media!"

"It's going to be very hard work! As for myself, I am going to take my son and go far, far away from here," Adem replied.

"I didn't say it's going to be easy! There will be people out there who don't like this idea of mine, and they might fight back! I thought about all that. As for you, you are free to go wherever you think is right for you! When you are ready, give me a call. I'll not let them off! None of them must escape justice! Remember what I said! I swear to that piece of bread, to light and to God! I'll not give my last breath, until I find them. You remember my phone number, don't you? Here it is once again: +381 (0) 38 22 55 88. I will set it up as a contact number. 'The Office for the Identification of the War Criminals' will be legal! Its activity will be legal, similar to an NGO."

"You figured all that out!"

"Not exactly! It needs a lot of time and people to establish. The Jews looked for Nazi war criminals for years. We have to do the same thing," Arben said enthusiastically.

"Okay, +381 (0) 38 22 55 88! I am writing it down so I don't forget." Adem took a pencil and wrote the number. "We have to keep in touch!"

"We have to look even in the rat's hole. KLA mentioned over two thousand criminals who are part of the police force, the army, the militant groups and civilian volunteers who have Albanian blood on their hands. The whole Serbian society has to divorce itself from Milosevic's politics of ethnic cleansing. Serbia has to change its constitution!"

"Hate is in their blood!" Adem said. "They need a blood transfusion first!"

"Maybe! But that comes after many generations, and I need to catch those bastards right now! Time is ticking away!"

Ermal didn't understand many things that Arben said, but deep in his heart he felt that Arben was right about going after the killers. That short conversation left him awake all night, giving him hope that payback would come with time. He felt great sympathy for Arben, even before the massive killings. He grabbed an orange from the small cabinet beside his bed and handed it over to the man, but Arben had already fallen asleep with a big smile on his face.

Adem noticed what Ermal did and felt warmth in his heart. He went out for a few minutes and came back with two plastic bags, one full of apples and one with oranges. He looked freshened up and energized from being outside. He placed the bags in Arben's closet and beamed at his son.

"Don't tell him I brought them for him," Adem said, as Ermal nodded in approval.

I promise you! We will find them even in the rat's hole. But it's not just a matter of those five criminals. The whole Serbian society has to face justice, starting from the first man of the state, the president of Serbia, Slobodan Milosevic.

Arben's words were easy to understand, but Ermal didn't have a clue how that could happen. It would not be too hard to catch the killers. First thing he was going to do when he became a grown man was to call Arben Morina for help on how to find Dragan Spasic and others who had killed his family. He just had to be patient until the war was over and wait to see what Babi was going to do next. It was not going to be that easy.

Not even a week passed and Arben went to the front line. He shook Ermal's hand, hugged his cousin Adem and with teary eyes made it to the exit door of the hospital. The wound on his leg was still not healed, but that didn't matter. Time had come for him to fight.

"Don't forget what I said. We will see each other there in a free Kosovo!"

Arben was barely standing with the help of his crutches. He waved at father and son and got on a four-by-four, which was driven by a KLA soldier. It would be several hours before they reached the border crossing of Cahan in Kukës. The military operation of KLA, which was coded "The Arrow" had just began.

* * * *

Ermal stayed in the hospital for almost two months. He kept thinking of 'The List' of the killers of his family that Arben was to draw up. Donika, one of the nurses at the military hospital, became very friendly with father and son. The day Ermal left the hospital for good, she invited them to stay for a while at her home, until they decided what to do next.

Donika lived in a three-bedroom apartment on the fifth floor of her building which was located in the northern side of the city's Oxhaku area. She lived along with her husband and two children: a daughter Ermal's age and a five-year-old son. Her husband Bashkim was a military officer in the Albanian Army and was born in the northern city of Tropoja, not far from the border with Kosovo. He was sympathetic to the plight of Adem and his son Ermal. Hundreds of Albanians from all over the country opened their doors to the Kosovo refugees and gave them food and shelter for months.

Staying at Donika's home was one of the best times for Ermal after the nightmare he had endured. The locals showed great hospitality to the million or so displaced people that poured in from war-ravaged lands. Their hosts tried to do the best they could, even with what little they had. The locals lived in poor conditions themselves, in small and narrow apartments where blackouts were common. Drinking water came through pipes only once a day. But their hearts were full with goodwill for their kin. Albanians felt it a national duty to welcome the refugees from Kosovo in their homes. Nurse Donika never forgot to give father and son a big smile and always asked Ermal if his wound still hurt. When they were sitting to have lunch or dinner, she filled Ermal's dish more than everybody's else.

Soon Ermal felt at home due to the peace and quiet in his new environment. Ermal became friends with Bora, Donika's daughter, who never left him alone and asked so many question about Kosovo. Once, as he was telling her what happened to his mother and three sisters, Bora's eyes filled with tears and she gave him a hug. Bora had long, black eyelashes and two little dimples formed in her cheeks when she smiled. She was definitely a pretty girl.

Their stay didn't last long. Some western countries, including Canada, had opened their doors to the refugees from Kosovo. There were over a million Kosovo refugees in Albania. Macedonia, France, Germany, Turkey, USA, and Canada had expressed their readiness to allow thousands of Kosovar refugees onto their soil. Two weeks after coming to Donika's place, Adem and Ermal were on a flight to Canada.

NATO bombing over Yugoslavia lasted seventy-eight days, from March twenty-fourth to June tenth until Serbian soldiers left Kosovo. The president of Yugoslavia, Slobodan Milosevic, signed the capitulation in Kumanovo city of Macedonia.

Three hundred refugees landed at a military base in Greenwood, Nova Scotia in one day, followed by another three hundred the next day. A total of ten thousand Kosovars arrived in different cities in Canada. Once they landed, all the refugees underwent a medical assessment and customs clearance. Then the Canadian army issued them clothing, food and lodging. Within a couple of days, they were moved away from the bases where they landed to another military barrack. Adem and Ermal were taken to a military base in Trenton, Ontario.

Canada had so much freedom, Adem couldn't get used to it. He still couldn't believe that the past was left behind, and he would time after time turn his head to see if someone from the Serbian secret service was chasing him and Ermal. As he walked hesitantly on the sidewalk, he noticed no one else, except local pedestrians and his own shadow, when it was very sunny. But it was a little weird at night. The ghosts of the loved ones who died in Kosovo appeared not just in his dreams, but in the living room as they were having dinner. Adem struggled to forget the pretty face of his wife Valbona and focus on ordinary things instead. But it didn't work. The dead were not letting him move on; they reminded him that their departure from this world was unfinished business. Adem kept pushing away his dark thoughts as much as he could, hoping that one day he would be free of the dead.

First they took shelter in a catholic church in Toronto. The priest, Stephen Aguinaldo, was very helpful and compassionate. As soon as he heard what happened to them, he was careful to keep their location a secret. When the journalists appeared at the door of the church to interview the boy and his father, the priest would tell them to leave, worried that they were still traumatized. There was a possibility that the Serbian secret service could find Ermal, the only survivor and witness to the massacre in his neighbourhood.

"If Ermal didn't have his father, I would adopt him," Stephen told one of the journalists.

The nuns brought food and clothes and prayed for them every night. The priest helped them find a small apartment in Etobicoke. He got in touch with The Albanian Canadian Association in Toronto, who helped them contact other Kosovars in Toronto. He took care of every detail of their settlement. He even accompanied them to No Frills and other discount grocery and department stores. Stephen took Adem once to a TD Bank branch and helped him to open a chequing account. His biggest concern was to find a job for Adem as soon as possible. He called several employment agencies for days; he even prepared a resume for Adem on his computer, but with no result. Most of the agencies asked for five years' Canadian experience.

As Adem lost hope, an employment agency called about a vacant job on a construction site in Brampton. Within a week Adem started work as a carpenter.

Ermal registered in an elementary school in Etobicoke, where he learned English and French. He adjusted slowly to his new homeland. Keeping himself busy, Ermal played soccer in his free time with the other kids in a field near the Humber River. To his surprise, he had a Serbian classmate, Boris, but he never told him his story in order to avoid any unpleasant questions. He played a lot with Boris on the school field and a few times they were on the same team.

Life seemed to go back to normal, until one day six months after their arrival in Toronto, a strange thing happened while he walked home. As he bounced the soccer ball on the ground, coming closer to the house where he lived, he heard some strange voices. He looked around, but didn't notice anything suspicious. He rushed to the house and went inside. He heard the voices again, but in a slightly lower tone. Feeling frightened, Ermal ran from one room to another. Things were in order. There was nobody there. He looked at photographs that hung on the wall. His three little sisters and Mami were smiling at him from the other world. Ermal felt empty and didn't know what to do next. Justice had not been done and the echoes of the last war had followed him. He moved his arm instinctively and rolled up his sleeve. There was just a little scar left from his bullet wound.

He felt relieved and tried to put the troubling thoughts out of his mind.

Ermal didn't hear the voices the next day, so he kept the strange occurrence secret. A week passed, a month, several months, and it looked like he was back to normal. There was only one thing he didn't like. All the coming days were gray and pretty much the same: they were filled with dark memories.

It was after six months that the ghosts of the dead again appeared in his dreams. Around three o'clock one morning, the shadow of his mother Valbona approached his bed and started to caress his hair. First he felt the tips of her fingers: soft, white fingers, which were shaking. He opened his eyes and turned on the lights. There was nobody around.

Ermal felt his throat dry up. He got up slowly from his bed and switched on the TV. It wasn't even Halloween, for God's sake! That night he watched TV until five o'clock in the morning. Deep in his heart he decided not to tell his father what happened. Adem would think that his son was going nuts and had some mental issues. Ermal let it go and decided to give himself time to get rid of the ghosts.

Christmas Day came so fast. There were so many vivid colours, and freshness in the air, so much love on the streets of Toronto, like he'd never felt in his entire life. People of different origins and backgrounds were wishing each other Merry Christmas. Even though he didn't celebrate Christmas, Ermal bought himself a Christmas tree in the No Frills supermarket and set it up in his home. He placed toys and pictures he had drawn of his mother and sisters on the green branches of the tree. When his father came home at night, he didn't say a word. Even though he was Muslim, the atmosphere in the city that day overcame all such considerations. "The religion of the Albanians is Albanianism. Be who you are and proud where you came from," Babi told him once, and he never forgot it.

The winter was harsh and passed slowly. Summer was quick and short and then it was Christmas again. It was a beautiful evening and a little snow whitened the streets like a curtain of joy. Ermal was home alone, making his Christmas tree beautiful. This time it wasn't a plastic tree, but a real one. His father Adem brought it home a day earlier. It was one of the little surprises that his father had for him.

Someone rang the doorbell nonstop. Ermal ran to open the door. Adem was standing on the doorstep and beside him was a woman from Kosovo, who was pulling a five-year-old boy by the hand. The boy had dark brown hair and deep black eyes. The woman was in her mid-thirties and had blonde wavy hair. Adem sounded emotional and his eyes had a strange, joyful sparkle.

"Hello, my name is Vjollca." She presented herself to Ermal and hugged him with affection.

Ermal was surprised to see his Babi bring a woman home. Everything happened so quickly and her visit was like a flash of lightning in a clear sky. Vjollca drank a glass of lemonade as the five-year-old sat shyly beside her on the sofa. Vjollca was not quiet for long. She asked how he was doing at school and invited him to her home, which wasn't too far from theirs. She hugged him again, took her son with her and left with a promise that she was going to visit them again soon.

Ermal watched her from the window as she and her son got in the car and drove away. Adem waited a few seconds and then sat beside his son.

"Vjollca is from Peja, you know. You probably saw her at the camp when we came to Toronto."

"No, I don't remember her," Ermal said abruptly.

Adem didn't like Ermal's sharp tone and was quiet for a while. He picked up the remote control and turned on the TV. He kept changing the channels, but didn't see anything interesting and left the remote on the table. Pretending to watch a TV program, he kept his eyes fixed on the screen.

"The Serbs killed her husband in front of her eyes and she has nobody here. I invited her for a coffee. That's all," Adem explained.

Ermal saw the plea in his father's eyes: an unspoken plea to Ermal that life didn't stop and had to go on after that terrible event that took place on March 24, 1999, back in Kosovo. His father was still young and there was nothing wrong with meeting someone and talking. Trying not to focus on the image of his gentle mother that was never far from his mind, Ermal muttered, "Ok! It's fine!"

Adem beamed at him and patted Ermal on the shoulder.

"Can I go outside to play soccer?" Ermal asked his father hesitantly.

"Go ahead. You don't have to ask me for that," Adem said, looking at him with wonder.

* * * *

Ermal kicked the soccer ball several times along the pavement before heading off to a convenience store. He bought a five-dollar Gold phone card with no connection fee and repeated Arben Morina's phone number in his head. He had memorized Arben's number since that day when he had met him at the military hospital in Tirana. Ermal dialed the number slowly and waited. His heart pounded against his chest. The phone rang. No one answered. He felt his face heat up with impatience, and grew dizzy. Suddenly the voice of an operator came through in English. Ermal struggled to catch every word.

"The number you are calling is not assigned. Please check the number and try again. This is a recording!"

What the heck! I guess I dialed a wrong number. Let me try one more time. I hope I dialed the wrong number, otherwise I'll be damned. Oh, shoot! My cell fell. Thank God it didn't break. Oh, perfect! There isn't even a scratch! I'll try again right now!

He grabbed the cell phone, which had fallen on the ground, and dialled the number again. This time he was very careful when dialling. A rough voice came on the line. Ermal recognized Arben's voice right away.

"Hello?"

"Hello! Is that you, Arben Morina?" Ermal asked, thickening his voice. A second passed. A very long second. Then two, three seconds.

"Yeah, it's me! Who's calling?" Arben's voice came and went with the poor connection.

"It's me, Ermal Bllaca! I'm calling from Canada. Hello, can you hear me?" he shouted with fear in his heart.

"Yes, I hear you! Ermal, how have you been? How are things in Canada? How is your Babi?"

"He's all right!" He paused. "How are you doing? Did you

make the List yet?"

"What List?"

"The List with their names!" said Ermal.

"Names of who?!" Arben asked. Ermal didn't speak. "Where is your father?"

"He's at home!" Ermal said, feeling disappointed. "The List of the killers we were going to go after."

"Say hi to your Babi from me! As for the List, I haven't done much. My advice to you is that you have to grow up first in order to talk about those things. I'll be here and I'll wait for you. Sounds good to you?"

"Okay," Ermal replied, heartbroken.

"Now go home and think how to get good marks at school. That is what you have to do," Arben said and hung up.

"Hello, hello?" Ermal couldn't believe his ears. Arben had hung up on him and treated him like a little child. His words echoed in his troubled mind.

Ermal sat on the bench beside the convenience store and leaned his head on both hands. His heart raced with a sudden thought: what if Arben found his home phone number and called Babi and let him know about Ermal's call? At least Arben had answered the phone, Ermal thought. At least Arben hadn't abandoned the idea of a List. He said that he was still working on it. He could have easily hung up on him right at the beginning or pretended that he didn't know what the hell Ermal was talking about.

Ermal felt a shiver go through his body. He imagined the anger of his father. He reviewed what Arben told him and concluded that he should be happy that Arben hadn't forgotten about his plan to find the killers and bring them to justice. How could Arben forget about the List, since his own family vanished that night in March of 1999? He shouldn't have told Ermal to grow up first, though! Ermal felt like a grown man already.

He went back home with his head down, thinking of how long he had to wait.

FOURTEEN

Vjollca visited them several times. Ermal wasn't sure what kind of relationship she had with his father, since she was always in a hurry to go back to her house, which was located in the same neighbourhood. Ermal didn't really care as long as she didn't become part of their small family.

He quickly forgot about her and got busy with his own life. During the day he went to school, and the afternoons were very tight: studying for a few hours, and during his free time playing soccer with his school friends. He found himself playing soccer more often. He even started to play hockey twice a week and his father registered him for karate once a week. Keeping himself busy with many different things made the days easier. Time passed quickly. It wasn't just his will, but Adem's hidden desire as well. There was less time to think of the past that way. But the memories were still there, sliding in right before he fell asleep, or before dawn, when he was waking up, making him shake in fear. These were the moments of the real, ugly truth, when he felt lonely and hopeless. These were the moments when he understood that no matter what he was doing, there was no escape from his memories. Many questions rose in his troubled mind, as he struggled to leave the past behind and focus on the future instead.

What would happen if Babi decided to marry Vjollca? The empty space that Mami left behind could not be filled. That vacant place was occupied by the ghost of his mother. Whatever Babi was doing to make his life better, it couldn't even approach the spot in his heart where he held the memory of Mami. It was impossible to accept Vjollca. Babi was still young and had a right to do whatever he wanted with his personal life, the same way he had the right to do something in order to make that heavy burden easier. Another voice whispered deep inside: that whatever Babi had with Vjollca, any kind of affair, was like cheating on his mother. It made Ermal feel abandoned.

Vjollca started to visit them more often, along with her son,

Butrint. Ermal tried to avoid any contact with her and the little boy, but Butrint kept wanting to play soccer with him outside. His vivid eyes begged him, so one day Ermal gave up and invited him to play. Other times, instead of soccer, they played PlayStation, killing hundreds of enemy soldiers with their controllers, while Babi sat beside Vjollca on the sofa and talked about Kosovo and their new life in Canada.

Their daily routine changed when a letter came from The International Court of Justice in The Hague. The international prosecutors had invited Ermal to testify in The Hague against the president of Yugoslavia Slobodan Milosevic. When Adem opened the letter, he felt his body shiver. He was surprised to read that his son was called as a witness against Serbia's top man Slobodan Milosevic. He tried to read between the lines without success, then handed the letter to his almost thirteen-year-old son, whose English was much better than his.

Adem stood still, listening as Ermal read the letter from start to finish. When he was done, Adem paced the room with both hands on top of his head. The past had caught up to the present to dominate the future. Ermal was designated a protected witness, "H91." He would sit only a few meters from Slobodan Milosevic himself, the former president and the commander of the Armed Forces of Yugoslavia, who had given the orders to the army and the police to 'punish' the Albanians through the coded operation "The Horseshoe."

Ermal would testify with all the little details about that event of March 1999, when five masked policemen entered the basement hideout and opened fire against five women and sixteen children. As Ermal finished reading out aloud, Adem noticed a light smile on his son's face. Adem nodded and pointed at the paper with his finger.

"Finally they are asking you to be a witness against those killers," he sighed. "We have to travel to The Hague soon. The time of justice has arrived," he said, eyes glowing with emotion. Adem had changed forever since that terrible incident. He realized that he'd become much more sensitive and would burst into tears, even when he was watching a movie. Tears rolled down his cheeks and his lower lip would quiver. He wasn't shy of his son seeing him cry. It wasn't the first time that he had cried like that. He wiped his tears with the back of his hand and hugged his son, held him tight to his chest for several moments. He kissed his son on the forehead, and grabbed his arms, as if to wake him from sleep.

"This is going to be the trial of the century! We still don't understand the importance of this moment, do we?"

"Maybe," Ermal answered, looking a bit confused and unsure.

"Don't be afraid! Prepare yourself to stand up face to face with that vampire. The mass killings in Kosovo couldn't have happened without his knowledge and approval. Life in prison would not be enough for the crimes his regime has committed. It would be too easy, a walk in the park, if he gets life in prison. May the Great Lord punish him with death in a prison cell," Adem said forcefully.

Adem was excited that Ermal was going to an international court as a witness. Ermal didn't show his feelings. He folded the letter carefully and placed it beside the TV.

* * * *

That afternoon Ermal tried to follow his daily routine of playing hockey at the arena on Dundas Street, but his attempts at normalcy were in vain. The next day he didn't feel like going to school. He dressed sluggishly then ran to the school on Varsity Road. His mind kept circling back to that letter. He found himself not paying attention to the teacher and in the evening not going to bed on time. He fell asleep after midnight and woke up very early in the morning. He realized that he could hardly wait for the day when he would get on the plane and stand in front of the president of Serbia.

Two travel tickets had been sent with the trial notice in the envelope, one for him and another for his father.

* * * *

The day arrived to fly to the appointment at The Hague tribunal. Father and son took a bus at Kipling subway station that took them to Pearson Airport. It was the first time that they were leaving Canada since they'd arrived as refugees three years ago. His father reached nervously for Ermal's hand and looked nervously around the airport for Serbian secret agents as they made their way to the boarding gate. He finally relaxed when they boarded the Canadian Airlines flight and took their seats.

Ermal was excited when the plane took off, and enjoyed the ten-hour flight. When they arrived at The Hague, a court police officer met them and ushered them to a hotel. The next day around two o'clock they arrived at the International Court of Justice. Everything happened really fast as Ermal saw himself sitting at the witness stand, inside a glass enclosure, right in front of the Serbian president Slobodan Milosevic, who without his official uniform looked like an ordinary man. Judge Schmidt, who sat to his left, saluted one of Milosevic's lawyers, Milan Djordjevic.

"You said you have a statement to make?" Judge Schmidt asked Djordjevic, who talked in Serbian. The voice of the translator came through Ermal's earbuds.

"Thank you, Your Honour. Just some information or notice to the Trial Chamber. We've done what you suggested that we should do regarding the H315 number, which was marked DFI ("don't force it"), and we forwarded the necessary documents. So I think that now we can proceed and tender this document into evidence. Thank you."

"There's no further difficulty with that, is there, Mr. Anderson?" This time Judge Schmidt addressed the prosecution lawyer Mr. Ralph Anderson, who was standing a few steps away from the defense lawyer, Mr. Djordjevic.

"Your Honour, I would need to consult with Mr. Shield. I believe that he may want to address this matter. If it's possible, I could provide an answer after the next break," the prosecution lawyer said.

Judge Schmidt nodded and turned to Ermal, who was sitting like a rock on his seat. The judge welcomed him and instructed him to swear before the court that he was going to tell the truth.

"I promise before Almighty God that the evidence which I shall give shall be the truth, the whole truth, and nothing but the truth," Ermal read the sworn testimony printed on a paper before him. He stared at the president of Serbia one more time before the judge, the prosecutors and the lawyers from both sides barraged him with questions. The face of the president remained impassive, as Ermal recalled the bloody incidents of that night in March of 1999.

Each trial session lasted four hours and continued for several days. His testimony was interrupted several times by the lawyers for the president, who were trying to make their point.

* * * *

"First of all on behalf of my client President Milosevic, let me express my sincere condolences to you for the loss of your mother and your three sisters. As I can see in your file, it is written that you described the weapon used as an AK-47. How did you know at that age that the weapon was an AK-47?" Djordjevic asked the boy.

"I just said 'machine gun.' I learned what type it was later on," Ermal said.

"Who told you that the gun was an AK-47?"

"I watched a lot of movies and that gun looked pretty similar to an AK-47."

"Have you watched a lot of movies even during that period of time?" Djordjevic asked him in a mocking voice.

"Yes, I watched a few movies," Ermal said with childish naivety. Ermal closed his eyes and tried really hard to go back in time to that awful night.

"What kind of uniforms did the armed persons wear?" the judge asked him and pointed to the big screen projected on the main wall. On the screen were shown a variety of Serbian uniforms: camouflage, blue, green, even white. Some of the armed men shown on the screen had masks on.

"Their uniforms were blue and all of them were wearing bandannas. They were policemen."

"Did you recognize any of them?" Judge Schmidt asked.

"Yes, the main shooter. He was our neighbour. I used to play soccer with his son. His son's name is Nenad."

"What was the name of the shooter?"

"Dragan Spasic!"

"How did you recognize him when he was wearing a mask?"

"I noticed his nose was bumpy and he was the only one who spoke a few words in Albanian. I recognized his voice too."

"How many policemen took part in the shooting?"

"Five policemen."

"Did you recognize the other policemen, other than Dragan Spasic?"

"No, sir."

The judge sighed, betraying frustration. "We need to identify all of them."

Serbian president Milosevic maintained a cold expression on his face throughout the trial. At the end of the session Judge Schmidt showed a video of Ermal being carried away to a military helicopter. The judge and the prosecution lawyer Mr. Ralph Anderson continued with more questions for Ermal: the identification of the persons shown on the video, who recorded it, how Ermal crossed the border, when the Serbian police confiscated the IDs, when he met his father Adem, how long Ermal stayed in the military hospital in Tirana, and a hundred other questions. Every single detail was important to the court.

Ermal struggled to recover from the fog of his memory all the names of the people he had met, the places he went, the faces of the dead, which were beginning to fade. With each day of questions, Ermal felt sadder, weaker and more tired. He was disappointed that just the head of the ruthless regime stood there, not the little guys who had pulled the triggers. Dragan Spasic and others were still free.

* * * *

Father and son returned to the International Court of Justice in The Hague four more times; but every time they went, they heard the same ordinary questions. It was like they were running back and forth in a closed circle. Ermal was only a thirteen-year-old boy when he went for the very first time to The Hague. Every two years he was invited to The Hague to testify, but never saw Dragan Spasic in the court or behind bars. There were only high-ranking Serbian officials and never the real little monsters who had pulled the triggers. Ermal acknowledged that the big monsters had blood in their minds; they had to be punished too. But they shouldn't forget the small evil ones who were still on the loose. The big monsters in the office gave orders to kill, but that was not enough to bring justice for those who had died. Why did the little fish escape the net? Where was Dragan Spasic hiding? Was there any attempt by Interpol or Serbia to catch him? What about the other policemen? Who were they? Where were they hiding?

Ermal and Adem had believed that the justice system would work and the perpetrators would get punished, but a lot of time passed and nothing happened. Eventually, Milosevic died in his cell, escaping a verdict. He had insisted to the end that he had no knowledge of what happened. Some officials had received from five to twenty years in prison. Vojislav Sesel, another warlord who had committed crimes against humanity in Croatia, was set free after a marathon twelve years of court sessions with the justification that his health had deteriorated. Hundreds of real criminals who had blood on their hands were still free and living a normal life wherever they wanted as though nothing had happened.

Even at his young age, Ermal understood that something was not working right in the justice system. International justice seemed to be a sham. Someone had to capture Dragan Spasic and the other murderers. Someone who was willing to do it. Someone who had a motive to risk everything for justice for the victims of the Gjakova massacre.

PART TWO

THE HUNTER

FIFTEEN

Fifteen years went by, but I still lived in the past, asking God what really happened. I couldn't understand why I was alive. Why didn't He let me die in the mass grave like the others? I would have been better off dead, ending this nightmare that I still lived.

God never answered my simple questions.

When I sat down with my father to celebrate my twenty-fifth birthday, I saw my Mami sitting with us. In my delirium, I was serving food for six people. Babi looked sadly, intently into my eyes. He was fighting with himself not to say anything. I was convinced my mother wasn't dead at all. She was the air itself that was coming in through the window. She was the breeze caressing my hair with her invisible fingers.

Hana, Trëndelina and Diona were the three angels that appeared on the ceiling of my bedroom every time cars passed by with their headlights on full beam. It was as if the world had ended at that exact moment, when I lost my family. As I was in the refugee line for Albania, I remember looking at the beautiful sky over the Accursed Mountains and finding my answer. God let me live so I could fulfill a final mission: I had to find their bones and give them a proper burial. But there was only one person who knew exactly where the graves were of the women and children gunned down in the basement in Gjakova—only one person on the face of the planet. That was the former chief of the local police of Gjakova city in Kosovo, who used to be our neighbour: Captain Dragan Spasic. He knew where the bodies had been taken.

First I had to call Arben Morina. I still had his phone number. This time I called him from home. There was nothing to hide. I was grown up enough to make my own decisions. Babi was sitting on the sofa, watching the morning news on TV. It was around ten AM on a Sunday, Babi's only day off, so we were spending some time together. I had no reason to hide anything from him. My plan shouldn't be a secret, I thought. He could probably help me in my mission.

"Who are you calling?" Babi asked.

"Arben Morina."

Babi looked at me strangely and hesitated for a moment. "Why?"

"He is our cousin, right?" I insisted.

"Of course! You're a grown man now. You can call anybody you like. You don't need my permission," Babi said and pretended to keep watching TV. It didn't last long. After a few seconds he asked, "Why do you have to call him anyway?"

I laughed. I was ready for his reaction. "Because..."

"Where did you find his phone number?" he interrupted me.

"I memorized it, from that day at the hospital."

"You still remember it from fifteen years ago?"

"Damn right!"

Babi slapped his forehead with surprise.

"What the hell! Why don't you say that both of us are in big trouble?"

"Not yet," I said sharply and dialed Arben's phone number. This time I got his number right. "Hello! Is this Arben Morina?"

"It is me! Who's calling?"

I recognized his voice; it hadn't changed. "Ermal Bllaca from Canada!"

Long pause.

"How are you? I hardly recognized your voice. What's happening?"

"You know it already. What about the List?"

"Eh, nothing much. There were some lists published in the daily newspapers, but not for the killings at Milos Gilica Street. The government is very weak here and my office doesn't have any support. Some of the Serbian criminals wore police uniforms and now work for Kosovo Police. Others even managed to become members of the Kosovo Parliament."

"No way. What about Dragan Spasic? Did you hear anything about his whereabouts?"

"Nothing! Call me again in a few months. We might be able to collect some information."

"OK, I am going to call you again. Thank you." I turned to

my father, who was standing beside me. "He was not able to do anything."

Babi sat down on the sofa, not showing any emotion. He finally said, "What do you need the List for?"

"I was thinking of killing them one by one, but I guess I can't do that before they tell us where they dumped the bodies," I said, looking him straight in the eye.

"You are not going to kill anybody! You are not a born killer!" Babi said sharply, looking alarmed.

"I said not before they show us where the mass graves are."

"I have only one son! Even if I had ten children, I wouldn't advise any of them to get a gun and go for revenge. If justice can't find them, God will take care of them for the rest of their lives. The faces of our loved ones will appear in their dreams. These kinds of people will never be at peace with themselves. I don't want to hear this story of revenge again. Period!"

I could tell from his shaking hands, reddened face, and teary eyes and from his loud, frightened voice that he had not shed the terror of the past. I hadn't seen my Babi like that for a long time. "Would you please promise me that you are not going after the List?" he pleaded.

"I can't promise you anything! I'm surprised that Arben Morina wasn't able to identify the killers at Milos Gilica Street in all this time. It shouldn't be so hard to find them."

"It's not just them! What about the other thousands of criminals all over former Yugoslavia and the rest of the world? Who is going to go after all of them?"

"I am only interested in those people in uniform who killed my mother and my three sisters. My List is short. I'm going to find them even if they are hidden in a rat's hole."

"You don't even have a list," Babi challenged. He sighed, then smiled a little and placed his hand on my shoulder. "How are you going to do this?"

"I'll go to Serbia."

"You don't need to go to Serbia. They might be in Kosovo, in Northern Mitrovica. Some of these criminals are members of the *Civilna Zastita Kosovske Mitrovice* (Civilian Protection for Kosovo's Mitrovica). Some of these criminals are even working in Prishtina Airport. They might be anywhere. A Serbian general was captured by Interpol in Argentina. They probably made it even here. It shouldn't be a surprise if you see them in our neighbourhood."

"Babi, what's your point?"

"You will risk a lot for nothing. Both of us are unable to do anything to catch or kill them. Let Interpol and The Hague Tribunal deal with them."

"They had plenty of time, more than fifteen years. What did they do? Tell me, Babi, what did they do? Those marathon court sessions against some officials drove me crazy!"

"They were not just 'some officials.' They designed the terror attacks for the little ones to carry out. You are not going anywhere without my approval."

"That we will see," I replied and went to my room. I didn't expect to have meaningless arguments with my Babi.

He knocked on the door, but I didn't answer. Babi didn't wait. He pushed the door open and came in. He sat on the corner of the bed and sighed in despair.

"So, do you really think that I personally don't want to go after them? I called Arben Morina too, but there's nothing he can do about it. Don't forget that he lost his family there as well. It's for his peace of mind too that he finds those killers. If you get caught in Serbia, you might end up in jail and no one, I repeat, no one can get you out of there. The worst is that you might get killed for nothing."

"I'll take the risk. I am not afraid of anything!"

"You are so naive and emotional and are doing your thinking without considering what you are up against. Who do you think you are and where do you think you are going? For a walk in the park?"

"If you want to help, you can do that. Otherwise I know what I am doing!"

"Calm down and stick with your life here. Don't fly too high. The higher you fly, the harder you'll fall. That is what I have to say!"

"Okay, I heard you."

"What does that mean? You aren't going anywhere without

my permission."

"I'm twenty-five years old! I don't need your permission," I said calmly, without looking at him. Babi didn't speak. He sighed deeply then got up and left the room. He slammed the door so hard the wall shook.

To my surprise, now that I had told my father, I felt more anxious than ever. I had to let it go for a while, until everything went back to normal and his temper eased. But I knew that even if I tried really hard to give him the impression that I'd changed my mind, he would find out sooner or later. Better to have Babi on my side, I decided.

It probably wasn't the best idea to go it alone anyway. I would need a back-up plan, a way out if something went wrong. I'd never thought that I would get caught or killed. I had to make sure one hundred percent that my plan would not fail. One person was not enough; probably three people would make a strong team. Maybe more.

I found Babi sitting on the sofa and sat beside him. He was holding his head with both hands, deep in thought. I patted him on the shoulder like a close friend. The whole situation was weird. I'd never talked so harshly to my father. It sounded like someone had died. The silence was so heavy.

"Babi, look. I am sorry. I'll do whatever you say from now on. My plan isn't perfect. We'll do it together. I'll go straight to Serbia and you can meet Arben Morina in Kosovo in the meantime. Both of you can cross the border and enter Serbia as woodcutters or something. We'll coordinate all our actions. What do you think about that?"

Babi shook his head in disbelief. He turned to me and looked in my eyes. He was trying to figure out if I'd really changed my mind, or if I was lying. He smiled a little. "The plan looks all right to me. I have only one son and I want to protect him like the light in my eyes. If you decide to go, let me know and we will go together. I am not going to let you go alone," he said and hugged me tight with his strong arms.

SIXTEEN

Babi got busy with his daily routine. As for me, I kept on working on my plan, which I'd had in mind for years. I had to start searching for the first name on the list, Dragan Spasic. I had a hard time identifying him since I didn't have a photo of him, but I remembered his face and I knew he was two meters tall. I became an expert on internet research and searched for related articles published in several newspapers around the world. The main newspapers wrote about the events in Gjakova in March and April 1999, but I needed to find one real person with a definite identity. I wanted to know where he was, his most recent picture, his current location, and what he was doing.

I missed my hometown of Gjakova. I missed my neighbourhood where I used to play as a kid. I wanted to visit my home, which was still standing, even after it had been burned. I wanted to touch its walls, blackened by smoke and fire. I had a dream to build my home all over again over the ruins. I wanted to visit the graveyard in the city where my sisters and my mother were supposed to rest in everlasting peace once we recovered their bodies. I wanted to put some flowers on the site of the mass grave where they may be buried. I missed my country Kosovo so much, which had only gained independence in 2008.

I waited for my Babi to come home from work. After he took a shower and was resting in front of the TV, I broached the topic. "Babi, don't you think we have to go to Kosovo for a short visit?"

Babi sighed deeply and placed his hand on my shoulder. He looked straight into my eyes, his own pleading in silence. I could feel his despair.

"There is nothing out there that can stop us from going to Kosovo, but don't you realise that our plan has to be a secret and be kept secret for as long as we can?" he said. "Let's say we went there, they saw us and we saw them, I mean our relatives. What's going to happen after? We have to go through all the details and then it'll be easy to plan."

"We might be able to get more information, and that is the

main purpose of the trip," I objected.

"We have Arben there to do that," he shot back. "In the meantime, you get going with your plan here," he insisted.

Deep in my heart I felt Babi was right, but I was so eager to see Mami and my sisters resting in the graves prepared for them in the graveyard where we would take their remains after they were found. I wanted to walk around the old neighbourhood where I grew up and had so many memories of my childhood. I squeezed the feeling back deep in my heart and turned back to my plan.

I kept drawing Spasic's image in notebooks, taking it with me wherever I went: when I sat down in the park; on the side of the street; on a bench in front of a supermarket; in my car. Anywhere. I drew his picture over and over again. First I drew his bumpy nose. I remembered that nose, and knew that it would help me identify him.

I read all the online Albanian newspapers. I was patient. I knew the time would come when the other victims would go after Dragan Spasic. His picture hadn't been released on the internet and Interpol didn't have him on its list of most-wanted criminals in former Yugoslavia. When I didn't see his picture, I realized that my plan could fail.

Serbia, in spite of being under pressure from the international community, did nothing to put these criminals behind bars. There were only one hundred and sixty-seven Serbians convicted by The Hague Tribunal for crimes all over former Yugoslavia. These included Milosevic, who topped the list, and most of the regional police commanders in Kosovo and Bosnia who gave orders or signed commands to have innocent civilians killed. The actual killers, the men who pulled the triggers, were still on the loose. The men who directed and fired the guns, the men whose hands were covered with blood, were all free, and were living a normal life. Enjoying their freedom.

Serbia didn't really want to catch Dragan Spasic. Serbia was not the right country to deliver justice for the victims of Kosovo, since it was the state, the system—the Serbian society itself—which was incriminated in the massacres. I had waited long enough for the Serbian state to be the first to seek justice. Dragan

Spasic was free. He was alive, enjoying life surrounded by all his loved ones, his wife, his son Nenad, and daughter Slavica, his mother and father, his father-in-law, and his brothers.

Where was Nenad, I wondered? Where was my old friend whom I used to play soccer with? Did he really know what happened to me, his school buddy? If he didn't know, what was his reaction going to be if he ever faced me, either by chance or by accident? What if I met him on purpose? I didn't really want to do that. If I did, I would blow my cover for good. I knew my goal: I had to go there and kill his father. That for me would be justice done. If I felt sorry for him, better that I didn't go there at all.

What about his sister Slavica, the first girl that I liked? Where was she? Did she ever get married? Did she ever ask anyone, either her brother Nenad or her father Dragan, where I was? Her blue eyes kept staring at me in my dreams, even as I saw myself shooting her father. A million times I imagined that scene, and every single time, I woke up. I looked up at the ceiling and prepared myself for the worst. I had decided to kill since I wanted to see justice done. I steeled myself and prepared for my mission.

Looking at Dragan's picture that I had drawn, I thought about Mami and my three sisters lying dead somewhere in a secret grave site. A mass grave had been found close to the city of Novi Pazar, but the remains of my mother and my sisters had not been found or identified, according to Arben. Our case was still without evidence of the bodies of victims.

I often wondered what had pushed Dragan into becoming a killer. And why did he hide their bodies? Perhaps the dead were chasing him. I wanted to understand his psychology. I started to read about the history of Kosovo. What pushed that soldier of Serbia to act like that? Where did he find the guts to pull the trigger on innocent civilians, on children and women? What did he drink early in the morning? Did he smoke opium, hashish, or pure insanity to have committed these atrocities?

I went deep into the history of these two peoples, the Serbians and the Albanians. The Serbs called the Albanians "people with tails," who had come from the mountains of Albania and had occupied Serbian lands. The Albanians, according to them, had "Turkish roots" that had been spread all over their land from the time of the Sultans of Turkey. On the other hand, the Albanians called the Serbs "Russians" who had grabbed the old Illyrian lands after they had migrated from the regions located beyond the Ural Mountains.

An inner voice whispered to me that whatever I had planned, it wasn't enough. The enemy was much more prepared. I was nobody, just a student who read history books. I was an inexperienced shooter who had never been in the front line; an unlucky dreamer, who dreamt with his eyes wide open in the middle of the day.

Time had come to call Arben Morina. What would he say to me? *Call me again in a few months!* Three months had passed. It should be enough for him to find something! Anything! He promised me that he would help me write the List. He promised me that he would help me find all five of the killers of his and my family even if they were hidden in a rat's hole! A promise is a promise. When an Albanian makes a promise, he keeps the promise. There is an old Albanian saying: "The Albanian man would kill his own son, if he promised to do so."

I dialled Arben's phone number. It was very early in the morning and there was no one else around. I took that day off work, just to make sure that I had the right time to make that very important phone call. I needed to be relaxed at home, and have plenty of time.

"Hello, is this Arben Morina?" I asked him impatiently.

"Hey, fella. How have you been?" Arben answered.

I cleared my throat. "Good! Do you have any news for me?"

"Guess what?"

My heart pounded in my chest. "What?"

"Finally I got him!"

"What do you mean?"

"I found Mister DS! He tops our List. He was seen hunting wild boars in southern Serbia. There's a place called Stara Planina."

"That's amazing! So why didn't you call to tell us the news?"

"I still need more information about him, and I knew you were going to call anytime soon. Now the problem is how to catch him and bring him before the court. Is your Babi there?"

"He's at work! I am afraid all three of us have to coordinate the plan. I can't go for it alone," I said.

"Glad you realized that. Your Babi has to come here and meet me. After I say 'yes,' you can go ahead with your plan."

"Sounds good to me."

"Are you in front of the computer?"

"Yes, I am!"

"I am sending you his picture by e-mail. Look at it so you have an idea who this guy is."

"Thank you very much. I'll do that right away."

I hung up and sat in front of the computer impatiently. For the first time after so many years I felt happy. I was shivering and couldn't get hold of myself.

I opened my e-mail and finally I saw him, Dragan Spasic. Arben's message mentioned two more names: Blago Stojkovic, the chief of the death group "The Jackals," and the third Nemanja Djuric, one of the militants who transported the dead to the unknown dump site. I sat on the sofa and cried like a little child. Finally I had some hope of avenging my mother and my three sisters. But what did Arben say to me? *The only problem is how to catch him and bring him before the court!*

"Hey, my dear cousin, that is not a problem at all," I murmured and wrote on a piece of paper the two words: STARA PLANINA. I searched on Google and found that there were two places called Stara Planina. I figured that I had to take my chance and just leave, and not wait for more details. I destroyed the piece of paper and threw it in the toilet, making sure that it disappeared after I flushed it. I waited for my Babi to come home. Now that I got the tip, I was more optimistic that things were going ahead according to the plan.

As soon as Babi came home that evening, I hugged him with joy and pushed him to sit in front of the computer. Babi looked at me with wonder.

"You look so happy today! What's going on?"

"I just spoke to Arben Morina. Dragan Spasic is hunting wild boars in a reservation in Southeast Serbia. It's called Stara Planina, but I am not sure yet which one Arben was talking about: Stara Planina I or Stara Planina II."

"Good! Now tell me what do you think. Are you ready to go to Serbia with so little information?" Babi asked me.

"Not yet. I'll let you know when I'm ready," I said.

"Very well!" Babi replied shortly. "I'll ask Arben for his advice about when is the best time that we can come and visit him in Kosovo."

Babi went to the bathroom to take a shower. I sat in front of the computer and started surfing. I struggled with myself. I found myself not feeling ready even for a simple visit to Serbia, never mind hunting down war criminals.

Babi was out of the shower quickly and with his head wrapped in a thick towel stood in the middle of the room.

"You better start learning Serbian a little," he suggested.

"I guess so." I nodded. Babi shook his head in disbelief and went to bed.

I surged the internet for information on how to learn basic Serbian language. I found an electronic Serbian-English dictionary to my surprise. I smiled a little and felt a warm feeling in my body. "*Now we are talking!*" I said to myself and started to practice. I kept practicing during my breaks and whenever I had some free time. Babi followed me at a close distance, pretending that he was not paying attention at all and shaking his head in disbelief behind my shoulders.

One day I couldn't be patient any longer, so I asked him about my Serbian.

"What do you think? Have I made any improvements at all?"

Babi laughed and sat beside me on the sofa. "You don't need to learn it perfectly. You probably just have to change your plan a little. For example, you can justify your lack of knowledge by saying that: 'I have forgotten my Serbian, since my parents passed away when I was just a child and I grew up in Canada,' or something like that!"

Babi's advice sounded reasonable. I guessed that I didn't have to present myself as speaking Serbian fluently. I could speak English most of the time and use Serbian words here and there.

"You're right," I said to Babi, but he didn't hear me; he'd

already gone to bed.

It wasn't just the language in which I needed practice. I had to learn how to use firearms. I registered for a target shooting class. I learned how to shoot from fifty meters away with only one hand. I went back to my plan, studying it in detail. I studied the picture of Dragan carefully. His hair had fallen out and he had wrinkles on his face. His picture was quite different from my sketches of him, with and without a hat, with and without eyeglasses, with and without a mustache, clean shaven, with a beard or bald. A hell of a job I had done, but now that I had his picture, I didn't need those sketches.

I took a driving course. I had to be well-prepared to face him. I woke up every morning at dawn, pulled on my pants and jersey, and ran along the Humber River. I was losing patience and my blood was boiling for revenge.

Dragan Spasic had just one weak point. He loved hunting and was at this time hunting wild animals in Stara Planina, in south-eastern Serbia, very close to the border with Bulgaria. I had to become a hunter just like him. I made my plan. I had to go undercover as a hunter from Canada who had a Serbian background. That way I could move around with my gun, looking for my prey.

I went to the Toronto Public Library at Jane and Dundas, and found an interesting book about the hunting grounds of Serbia. There were over three hundred and twenty hunting camps in Serbia, but I had to find out which one Dragan Spasic frequented to satisfy his desire to kill living creatures. I read about mammals in Serbia: the red deer, fallow deer, white-tailed deer, and roe deer.

Hunting tourism in Serbia had strict rules about crossing borders, travelling to the hunting grounds, obtaining weapons and ammunition licenses, and qualified guides, as well as veterinary licenses, and other requirements for exporting game.

A hunter can hunt and train hunting dogs in hunting grounds only with the mediation of an authorized agency which has signed a contract with the user of the hunting ground, I read on one of the websites about Serbian hunters.

I rechecked the whole plan in detail. Something very

important was missing. I needed legal travel documents in order to be able to get into Serbia. Otherwise I would end up in trouble with the authorities. I struggled with myself for more than a week, but I couldn't find a solution.

I was taking a shower one day when an idea came to me. I had to obtain a fake passport, assume someone else's identity and identification papers. I needed all applicable licenses, the game seals, the validation tags, and even the certificate to hunt wild boar. I had to comply with the federal firearms regulations. I decided to be a real hunter. I had no choice. One little mistake would cost me much more in the field. I had to take a real training course in hunting in order to get used to handling a gun. I had to behave like them – be one of them.

I had to play simple, to play safe. Being legal in the eyes of Serbian officials was crucial to my game. For hunting in Ontario, I needed a class H1 Outdoors Card, which would allow me to go hunting with all the methods permitted under the Fish and Wildlife Conservation Act. If I really wanted to have that card, I found out that I had to provide proof of passing *both* the Ontario Hunter Education Course exam and the Canadian Firearms Safety Course exam.

The problem was that I needed to obtain them under someone else's identity.

To practice speaking Serbian, I started to visit the Serbian night clubs in Toronto, one after another. When someone asked me something, I always answered back in Serbian. Finally, I found an interesting person in a club called "The Belgrade," who looked pretty similar to me.

I met Sashenka, a twenty-four-year-old girl who was half-Russian and half-Serbian. I danced with her almost every weekend, until one night I came pretty close to the Serbian guy who looked like me. He was the same height as me, but his hair was blond and his eyes blue. Though I had black hair and brown eyes, I had the same nose as him and almost the same features. The Serbian guy was dancing with another girl as I was going around him on the dance floor, holding Sashenka in my arms.

I looked at him and asked him if we could change our partners for a short dance. He laughed and let his girlfriend dance with me, and he danced with Sashenka. After the music was over, I invited him for a drink at the bar. His name was Bogdan Tadic, and since he was born in Toronto, he could hardly speak Serbian. I told him that I lost my Serbian roots as well, and wanted to get in touch with the Serbian community.

The next Friday I saw Bogdan once again. I went there with Sashenka. After several dances with her, it was Sashenka who spoke to his girlfriend first. Bogdan invited me to the bar, where we had a few shots of Sambuca, White Russian, Sex on the Beach, and a Screwdriver. He was drinking like hell. Nursing my own drink, I paid a lot of attention to the environment around me, making sure that I didn't blow my cover.

Bogdan got drunk really fast, and I was obliged to help him get home after two o'clock in the morning. His girlfriend Natasha and my girl Sashenka gave me a hand to lift him and put him into the taxi. The four of us went to his apartment on Eglinton Avenue East. His things were all over the place, and from what I could see, I judged that Bogdan was heavy into the night life scene.

Even after he became conscious, Bogdan grabbed a bottle of vodka from the side table and started to drink like he had never drank before. The entire world was closing down around him, but he didn't know how to stop. He pointed to another alcoholic drink, *Slivovica*, on top of the fridge and invited me to drink with him. I couldn't believe how much he could handle, as I was trying really hard not to get drunk. In a couple of hours all of them ended up drunk, passing out on the couches.

I was still sober. I got up slowly and kept glancing back, checking every single one of them to see if they were really in a deep sleep. I put the radio on, and increased the volume, and they still didn't wake up. Feeling relieved, I started to check his bureau drawers, and in a few minutes I was able to find his passport. I put it in my pocket and left in silence. Bogdan had assured me earlier that he had no intention of going to Serbia and that he didn't have any plans to leave Canada any time soon either.

I went home and checked myself in the mirror, comparing my face with his. I realized that I had to change my hair colour and buy blue contact lenses for my eyes. I had to adjust my appearance, making myself look exactly like him.

My Babi kept watching every single change without interfering. He laughed really hard when I tried the contact lenses once and put them back in the drawer. I tried to explain to him that I was going to change my hair colour because I was seeing a girl who liked blond hair. He smiled at me, patting me on my shoulder without saying anything.

I cut my hair and dyed it blond. I found a men's magazine and with that in hand, I went to the nearest barber shop and pointed to the picture. One of the models had the same hairstyle as Bogdan. After I was done with my hair, I went on the internet and searched on Google for any hunting clubs located in Serbia. A huge list came up on my screen.

I looked for hunting clubs in southern Serbia. On the site for a Serbian hunting club called Alfa, I saw Dragan Spasic's image as one of their staff members. At the sight of him, my body shivered with strong emotion.

I made a reservation through Alfa's website. The hunting dates were considered booked after a confirmation e-mail. I went to an internet cafe and opened a fake account on Yahoo under the name of Bogdan Tadic and sent the e-mail. I had to do one more thing: I had to make the payment. I couldn't use my banking card, or my credit card. I put Bogdan's passport in my pocket and went to the nearest money exchange in Toronto and bought a Titanium+ credit card with cash. There it was: my new identity on the credit card with an expiry date on it. With the same credit card, I made the payment to the agency and that was it: in a matter of seconds I got an official receipt from the Serbian Hunting Club, a pre-form invoice with time and date and a logo. I didn't even need to pay the full amount, only fifty percent of the planned hunt. The rest I could pay at a later date before arrival. That meant I had a lot of time to get some more cash and buy another Titanium card from another money exchange location, just in case I needed it on my long trip.

I checked my reservation carefully, every single detail: my new name, my new date and place of birth, my passport number – my type of hunting permit. Dragan Spasic hunted boars. I had to hunt wild boars as well. I figured I would get in touch with him within a week, so I requested a seven-day hunting period on the form. I had to find accommodation, a hotel where I could stay.

Stara Planina was the closest hotel to where Dragan Spasic worked with Alfa. I had to provide information on my weapon, the type, the serial number and the calibre. I left that information blank, and wrote that I was not bringing any gun with me and that I was expecting that the agency would give me a gun. I put down that I needed a hunting rifle, minimum caliber 7x57 and minimum bullet weight nine grams. I had done some research and found out what type of gun was needed to kill a wild boar in accordance with the hunting laws of Serbia.

They needed a fax and a telephone number. I wrote the phone and the fax number of the internet cafe Romeo in downtown Toronto, where I used to hang out most of the time. But all these little steps were not enough. Besides the passport, I needed two more identification papers, a hunting license and a permit to carry weapons. I spent a lot of time on the internet and finally found an example of what a hunting license would look like. I had to know. I was even able to find an original copy of a gun permit posted on the Ontario Hunting website.

I opened Adobe Illustrator and designed both the hunting license and gun permit identical to what I found on Google. But I was not happy with the results. They had to be real. All the documents had to be real, I concluded. There was no fooling the system.

With Bogdan's passport I registered myself in a hunting course. With the same passport I was able to get the hunting permit. With a little patience, and with Bogdan's passport and P.O. box address, I passed the Education Course Exam and obtained the license to hunt permit.

There were other details I had to keep in mind. As a tourist hunter, I had to specify the number of heads I wished to shoot—apart from the head of Dragan Spasic, I thought to myself. I could shoot wild boar only with permission, but to shoot Dragan I didn't need anyone's permission, not even from God Himself. I just needed an invitation letter from the hunting agency, and as soon as I got that I could prepare for my departure.

I decided to contact the Serbian Hunting Club in Toronto. I dialled their number and a female voice answered in a matter of seconds. I presented myself as Bogdan Tadic, Canadian-born of Serbian descent. The lady on the phone was very nice. She told me her name was Lepa, and that I should come and see her. I made an appointment to apply to become a member of their association. I gave her a P.O box number for my mail.

I took the subway and got off at Eglinton Station, where their main office was located. I kept Bogdan's passport with me all the time, like it was the most important thing in my life.

When I went upstairs to the fifth floor on the elevator, I saw Lepa. She was about twenty years old. She was satisfied with my idea to visit my homeland, Serbia. She was beautiful and sexy, but she kept a professional manner.

"Did you pass your hunting exam?"

"Yes," I said.

"Do you have a hunting permit, Mr. Bogdan?"

I took out both legal documents from my pocket and placed them on her desk. She studied them and did not hesitate to sign a letter of recommendation for the Serbian authorities. I handed Bogdan's passport to her and she wrote an official paper for me right away, signed and sealed on behalf of the Serbian Hunting Club of Toronto. She took a picture of me with her camera and glued it on top of an ID issued by her Association. I shook her hand amicably, feeling triumphant.

I went back home, avoiding my father as much as I could, and spending a lot of time looking at myself in the mirror. To be Bogdan Tadic was not easy, but so far, so good, I thought. I was the real Bogdan Tadic from then on, a Serbian who was born in Toronto, who was going to hunt pigs in Serbia.

I waited impatiently for Babi to come home from work. I felt deep in my heart that finally things had moved forward. I was ready to get on the first plane to Belgrade.

"Babi, I think I am ready now," I announced to him as he walked in.

"Are you sure about that?" He studied me carefully.

"Totally."

"Well, not quite yet! I need to go to Kosovo first and make sure that everything is all right. Then you can book the flight to Belgrade. What do you say?"

"Sure, you can do that," I replied, heartbroken.

"Okay then!" Babi sounded relieved. "In the meantime, I'll spread the word to my friends that I'm going to Hamilton for a few days to build a cabinet worth about thirty thousand dollars. Since they know that I am a cabinet-maker by profession, most of my friends are already used to me getting jobs far away from Toronto."

I nodded. There was no way I could change his mind. I tried to put myself in his shoes. He really wanted me to be safe before I put my first step out there.

First thing in the morning I called Sultan Travel and booked a direct flight to Kosovo for my Babi. As for me, I had to wait until he gave his 'A-okay.' The next day I took my Babi's car and drove him to Pearson Airport. Babi took just his regular clothes with him, a small suitcase and nothing else. I hugged him for the last time before he checked in.

"We have to keep in touch all the time, no matter what!" he said to me at the gate. "We have to know where you are, otherwise it will be very difficult for us to intervene. That's the only reason I am leaving before you."

"I know! Call me as soon as you arrive," I said with a big smile on my face. I could see in his eyes that he was still worried.

As the Canadian Airlines jet lifted off, I went back to my car, thinking for the very first time that extra precautionary steps could never hurt.

SEVENTEEN

After an eleven-hour flight and four-hour delay, Adem Bllaca finally arrived at Adem Jashari Airport in Prishtina. As he passed through the gate, Adem saw his cousin Arben Morina, who ran up to him and hugged him. Adem choked up and couldn't speak as emotions welled up in his throat and he could hardly breathe.

Adem noticed that his cousin hadn't changed much in all the years since they last saw one another, except that his hair had thinned on his forehead and had turned grey at his temples. After a short pause Adem tried to break the tense silence and started to ask him about all his friends and relatives. As they walked outside toward a cab, he looked around for any signs of the ravages of the 1999 Kosovo war. They were not there, but instead only deep in his heart. The bombarded rooftops had been totally repaired and the bystanders on the road seemed well-dressed and happy. Prishtina city was crowded with smiling youths. Adem noticed that the cab had the word *Jakova* painted on both sides. That was the old name of his hometown Gjakova. To his surprise Arben was the cab driver.

"The people might look happy, but there are no jobs here," Arben said. "Everybody wants to leave. I've had this part-time job as a cab driver for some time now. Do you have any immediate visit that you want to make?"

"Take me straight to the graveyard of the city. I want to see if they are ready," Adem replied, still struggling with his emotions. Arben pushed the gas pedal. He asked him about his new homeland Canada, where he'd immigrated fifteen years ago. The emotions still blocked his throat, so he gave very short answers most of the time.

Adem felt like he was coming back to another world which he had left many years behind. He felt deeply disturbed as they drove to Gjakova. In less than an hour they arrived in front of the gate of the graveyard. It was very close to dinner time and there were very few visitors: a handful of old women dressed in black from head to toe and some kids. Adem lowered his head to avoid eye contact with anyone who might recognize him. He was still heaving with emotion. He was timid, not because he didn't want to meet his friends from the neighbourhood, but the tears could betray him in front of them at any moment and a man crying was against his culture. A man is just a piece of stone that can never break apart. A man is born to face everything and never give up.

They reached four empty graves: a grave for his wife Valbona and a grave for each of his daughters, Hana, Trëndelina and Diona. He clenched his teeth to keep himself under control and not to burst into tears. He knelt down and kissed the gravestones one by one and stayed a few minutes in silence. The graves looked beautiful. They were built in a perfect line right beside each other and were covered with crowns of fresh colourful flowers. The money that he sent to his cousin Arben had not been wasted. The only thing missing was the bodies of their loved ones. Adem wondered if that day would really come when he could bring his dead loved ones home. Would they ever be identified? Were they going to rest in everlasting peace?

He walked a little further and stopped in front of the graves of Arben's relatives. There should have been the remains of Bajram Morina, the father of Arben, who gave his last breath defending his *Kulla*, along with the other graves of Arben's wife and two little daughters. They were empty as well. He leaned toward them with respect and looked around.

There was a whole miniature city of its kind all in marble, lying in front of him. A unique graveyard. A graveyard which was waiting for its occupants, who had disappeared in unknown grave sites. The whole city's graveyard was well maintained. "*Thirrjet e nenave*" (The Mothers' Appeal) Association, "The Veterans of KLA Association" and private businessmen had sponsored the renovations of the site. Over fifteen years had passed since the war had ended, but it felt like the killings had taken place just a few days ago. There was no sense of peace and restful silence in this graveyard. A slight breeze of the evening was blowing, bringing to his ears the forgotten voices of the dead.

Ah, you have come already! I knew you would come! I knew you would not leave our graves empty. We shall never be in peace if you don't find our bones. The foreign land will not absorb us if you don't bring us here! How can we be quiet when these graves are waiting so many years for us?

It was just the evening breeze. The world of the dead doesn't exist. If you are gone, you are gone and that is it. He felt his spine shivering and struggled to stand up and face reality. They got back in the cab and entered Milos Gilica Street, the same street he left fifteen years ago. There were no more tanks, no Serbian army or police. Most of the homes had been restored and renovated. More than half of the city had relatives working abroad, and everyone had tried to cope with the grave wounds of the war. It seemed that with the exception of the graveyards and broken memories, the signs of war were not there anymore. His feet stopped in front of his house. It had been rebuilt with the money that he sent Arben every couple of months. The house had been put up for rent more than a year ago. He touched the walls with nostalgia and his eyes filled with tears. The ghosts of the loved ones appeared in every single step. Before he could erupt in sobs again, Adem felt a hand touching him gently on the shoulder.

"Let's go. Dafina just called me to say that she made a nice dinner and is waiting for us to come," Arben said in a hushed voice, as if he was afraid he would startle his cousin. Adem shook his head as if he was trying to wake up and followed his cousin's steps. As they went back to the cab Arben looked like he wanted to ask him for something.

"What's the matter?" Adem asked.

"I was wondering if you called your son yet."

"Not yet."

"Here, call him."

Adem took the cellphone from Arben's hand, thanking him with a big smile. "Hello, Ermal? How are you? Yes! I arrived over an hour ago. Arben is saying 'Hi!' We are going to his home right now. I'll let you know when you can go on with your trip," he said shortly and hung up.

The three-story *Kulla* had been rebuilt over the ruins of the old building the old man Bajram had defended with his life. The living room, or "*the chimney room*," as they called it, was designed in every detail as it was before, when he visited them for the last time.

Arben's wife Dafina welcomed them warmly as soon as they entered the house. The whole building smelled of *byrek,* which was made of thin layers of dough, brushed with butter and filled with spinach and feta cheese, cooked in a skillet in the wood oven that was set up in the backyard. Adem couldn't remember the last time that he had tried *byrek* baked under a metal cone and covered with glowing coal. As they sat around the table to have dinner, Dafina went back and forth, bringing all they had for their special guest. Arben had married Dafina three years ago and they had one son.

The evening went smoothly around the fire, bringing back to life all the memories of their loved ones, who lost their lives during the 1999 war.

The next day Adem woke up before dawn. Two more hours passed, until he noticed that Arben was awake. Even though he was still feeling tired, he was too worried to fall asleep again. He feared that Ermal was getting into a very dangerous adventure with his trip to Serbia. He sat beside the window sill with a grim look on his face and gazed outside, as if he was searching for a way out. It was the same window sill of the second floor apartment where the old man Bajram supported his Mauser rifle and took aim at the Serbian army and police who surrounded the house. He was so deep in thought that he didn't notice Arben saluting him, or even Dafina, who placed a steaming espresso cup for him on the dinner table.

"Hey! How did you sleep? Did you freshen up yet?" Arben asked. Adem didn't speak. He sipped the coffee in silence. Adem noticed that Arben winked at his wife Dafina secretly, telling her to leave the room. He heard him clearing his throat intentionally. "Are you going to talk to me or not? What is your problem? Do I have to use pliers to take your words out?" Arben picked on him.

Adem forced a smile and turned to him. "All this work is worthless," he finally spoke. "I'm afraid that it would be a mistake to let Ermal go to Serbia. He might get killed. He is just waiting for my signal to get on the plane." He sighed and covered his face in despair with his wrinkled, tanned hands.

"Call him and tell him not to go, as simple as that."

"It's not that easy. He's been training for so many years, waiting for this day to come. The graves are waiting for their dead. On top of that, I gave him my *Besa* (word of honour)."

"You shouldn't have given him your *Besa*!"

"It's too late now to say that." Adem sipped the last of his espresso and stretched his arms, making himself comfortable in the chair. He liked espresso without sugar and its bitter taste shook him free of a little of his lethargy. "The plan has to be professional and fully detailed in order to be successful. Do you think that this operation will end with success?" He stared at Arben, waiting for his opinion. "Why do you hesitate to answer me? I guess that it's not a plan with a chance of success? Better Ermal doesn't go there at all. I have only one son and I don't want him to get involved in danger."

"Tell me anything that can be a hundred per cent sure."

"I'll never forgive myself if something were to happen to him."

"Don't even say that! Never foresee the worst! Me too, I don't agree with Ermal about this adventure. It's crazy just to imagine it, but I have a back-up plan, a way out. We are going to be there for him. You and I can do this. Here, come and sit with me in front of the computer."

Arben got up and put the computer on. A map of Serbia appeared on the screen. Adem grabbed the mouse and zoomed in. Arben pointed to one of the locations.

"Do you see this circle here? This is *Shpella e Arushës* ("The Cave of the Female Bear"). We have to enter Serbia as woodcutters right after midnight. In case we face the border patrol, we are going to say that we entered illegally. We will meet a former fighter of UCPMB at *Shpella e Arushës.* The only way to get there is to ride through a narrow path up the hill at *Bjeshka e Qershizës* ("The Mountain of the Cherry Tree"). It's a long and difficult trip, over rough, rocky ground. We are all going to use light sport motorcycles, which are used by the local alpinists. Both of us will join a group called *'Alpinists of Presevo,'* which in fact are former members of the armed Albanian group UCPMB. They will lead us to the cave where two hunting rifles are hidden. As soon as we get the rifles, we will go to Stara Planina. There are two Stara Planina. Stara Planina I is located in Bulgaria and Stara Planina II is in Serbia. We will be hiding around the location of Stara Planina II. If we are seen by a patrol police, which I doubt will happen, we will present ourselves as hunters. We will dress like them, behave like them; we'll even have hunting rifles, so they won't be suspicious. You can call Ermal, but only when we arrive there first. What do you think about the plan?" Arben was eager to hear his opinion.

"Is this the best plan we have?"

"That's the only way we can reach the hunting ground of the wild boars. Three of us, you, Ermal, and me, are more than enough to catch Dragan Spasic, who will show us where the mass grave is."

"When can we leave?" Adem asked him impatiently.

"Right after midnight. First we have to meet Captain Buja, one of the former commanders of UCPMB in Presheva, who will give us fake IDs of Albanians living in Medvegja. He will show us the details on the map where we can cross the border," Arben explained.

"Where is this person?"

"We can meet him here in Gjakova. We can leave now." Arben got up from his chair and put his jacket on.

"How do we know that Dragan Spasic is still in Stara Planina II?"

"I have it from Kosovo Intelligence Agency. I have a friend working for them."

"So, they know what we are doing..."

"Not exactly. But no one can stop us from finding war criminals. It's supposed to be their job. They can do anything they want and Ermal can try on his own. You and I are not letting him do this mission alone."

"That is quite right!" Adem agreed and followed Arben to the cab, which was parked in front of the house.

EIGHTEEN

I arrived at Belgrade's airport after a twelve-hour flight. My body felt sluggish since I couldn't sleep at all during my flight. It was my first time in Belgrade, the capital of Serbia, which was one of the most beautiful cities in Europe. 'One of the most beautiful cities,' of course, since the work and financial contribution of six former republics and two autonomous provinces of former Yugoslavia went into keeping that city shining.

Nicola Tesla Airport was a little bit smaller than Pearson Airport, but it was well maintained and clean. Seven years ago, the airport was named 'Tesla' after the scientist who had many inventions in the field of electronics. The statue of Tesla was three meters tall and gave me the impression that it was erected for some political purpose. Maybe it was an attempt by the Serbian government to improve its image.

Dragan Spasic is still on the loose. That is why I am here. I tried to forget about him for a moment and instead looked around like a tourist. There were two terminals in the airport and I was at T1. Both terminals were located next to each other and were connected through a hallway. I had some time to go to the three restaurants, Aviator, Boeing, and the Business Club Lounge. When I sat in the Aviator, I saw a tall man who looked very much like Dragan. I didn't turn my head, just sat at a distance from the man. He had dark glasses on and a grey jacket. I got a newspaper in English and pretended that I was reading it. I walked between the tables and went closer to him. It wasn't him, just some guy who happened to look like him.

I felt relieved and stood in line. There were passengers from all over the world, but mostly Serbians who took Air Serbia to their homeland with pride. To my surprise, most of the customs personnel were attractive women. I showed the passport to the customs officer and waited in silence. The female officer gave me a sweet smile. Her eyes were full of light. I had the impression that she liked me. Her hair was blonde and her eyes deep blue. I had to be on my guard. It would cost me big time if

I let down my guard and got arrested and ended up in jail for false identification and impersonation. I forced a smile on my face and looked straight into her eyes.

"It's a beautiful airport," I said to her, showing a lot of warmth and respect in my voice.

"Is it your first time visiting Serbia?" she asked.

I had one-tenth of a second, but I didn't know what to answer. When I checked the passport a few days ago there weren't any stamps by customs officials. I guessed it was the first time I was coming to Serbia.

"Yes, it is!" I answered quickly. Bang! It was the right answer. I could tell from her eyes when she was checking the passport I had given her.

"What's the purpose of your visit?" she asked me again. "Do you have any relatives here?"

"No, I just came for hunting."

"Do you have any letter of recommendation from a hunting association?" she asked.

I showed her the letter that Lepa had given me.

"Where are you going?" she asked me again.

"I'm going to hunt in Stara Planina. Our club in Toronto showed us some pictures of this hunting ground. It looks amazing," I said to her.

Stara Planina II was the hunting ground where Dragan Spasic was last seen, not more than a month ago. He had been holding a gun and posing beside a roe deer.

"Oh yes. That habitat has roe deer, wild boar, bears, wolves, wheatear partridges, wild pigeons, woodcocks and lots of other game to hunt. You are going to have a lot of fun!" she said.

"That is what I came here for," I answered and smiled.

I handed her a booklet about the hunting grounds of Stara Planina II, which I got at the Serbian Hunting Club in Toronto. The booklet was written in both languages, English and Serbian.

"Where do you plan to stay when you arrive there?" the officer asked.

My answer was ready, right on the tip of my tongue. I handed her a printed list from my computer with the names of the hotels in the surrounding area. The female officer looked satisfied with my list. Hunting in Serbia is a big deal. I showed her a Serbian magazine filled with pictures of monasteries nearby, pointing to one of them, St. Jovan Bogoslov, which had been built in the fourteenth century. I had studied the area well. There was an artificial reservoir called Lake Zavoj where I would go hunting. The River Toplodolska was nearby.

I would go hunting there as well, if Dragan Spasic was going to be there.

I would go to the Zvonacka Spa if Dragan went there. I imagined the bathtub filled with his blood, and my eyes gleamed with revenge. I was eager to go there immediately.

The customs officer read the list carefully and gave me a sweet smile.

"A couple more things..." she added. "Do you have a hunting license with you or permit to carry a weapon?"

Without even moving a single muscle on my face, I struggled to keep the same innocent smile. I pulled both documents from my handbag and handed them to her. One second, two, three seconds passed. The female officer looked at them without any suspicion and handed them back to me.

"Did you bring a gun with you?" she asked me.

I knew that I could have brought a gun with me, but it would just cause extra trouble. "I decided to get the gun from the agency here," I said, struggling not to show any kind of emotion. My answer was quite true.

I felt my excitement rising. I was just a few hours away from being face-to-face with Dragan Spasic. Was it ironic, a random wish that the custom officer gave me? It was going to be a hell of an adventure for sure. I imagined Dragan with a gun in his hand as he shot wild boar. What if he found out that I was undercover, that I had come to seek revenge? What if something didn't go exactly like I had carefully planned? So far everything was going so well. I took the custom officer's wish for a good trip to heart.

"I wish you a very good hunting trip," she said and let me pass.

"Thank you very much," I said and put all my papers back into my handbag, giving her a big smile.

Very good hunting I need indeed, I thought, and rushed to the exit door.

A representative from the Hunting Agency "Alfa" was supposed to wait for me at the airport. I looked around and noticed a man around thirty at the exit door of the airport, holding a paper on which was written 'Bogdan Tadic.'

Bogdan Tadic is me from now on. I can't forget that, I said to myself.

I saluted him and spoke to him in English. He introduced himself as 'Danillo', squeezed my hand and pointed to his car, which was parked on the side of the road. Within an hour I was in one of the luxury rooms at the Falkenstainer Hotel in New Belgrade. I threw myself on the double bed and lay upside down, feet toward the headboard, without moving at all for several minutes, trying to relax and forget where I was for the moment. So far everything had gone smoothly, so smooth that I started to doubt the whole trip. When I pinched myself, I realized that I was not dreaming. I took a long shower and got out of the bathtub only when I felt I could fall asleep.

After I had slept a few hours, I left the hotel to visit Belgrade, the White City, which had been built where the Danube and Sava rivers crossed. I walked the streets filled with people and held my breath in front of the building called Palace Albania which was built during the Second World War in place of a coffee shop with the same name. The former coffee shop owner named his business in honour of Albania, which during the war didn't let Serbian soldiers die from hunger as they were pulling back.

I found Albanian names all over the old city, especially the street called "Skenderbegova Ulica." That street was named after the Albanian national hero, Scanderbeg, in 1896 when the Serbs thought that he was Serbian by origin. I sat in one of the coffee shops in Skadarlija, the most beautiful part of the city, named after Shkoder, the northern city of Albania. I took a deep breath and decided not to follow the Albanian roots of Belgrade, otherwise it might look suspicious. There were over eight thousand Albanians living in Belgrade. I better avoid any kind of contact with them as well, in case someone realized that I was Albanian myself. It would be better if I pretended I didn't speak the Albanian language at all.

The next day Danillo picked me up in front of the Falkenstainer Hotel at Boulevard Mihajla Pupina and Blok 11a. I had had a good sleep the previous night and my body was light and energetic. The time had come to hunt.

"*Doberdan*," Danillo saluted me in Serbian and invited me into his car.

"*Doberdan*," I saluted him back and watched him carefully. I didn't see any sign of doubt in him. My accent was satisfactory.

"Do you speak Serbian at all?" Danillo asked me in a friendly voice, opening the door of the car.

"Nothing at all. My Babi was Serbian, but he passed away when I was just a year old."

"That's all right. I speak English a little bit, so it's not going to be a problem. Sorry to hear about your father." Danillo turned his head back, giving me a sad look. He seemed like a nice man, in his thirties. He had a short moustache and long brown hair. He sat behind the wheel of the Zastava, I sat in the back seat, enjoying the view.

"Are there many Serbs in Toronto?" he asked me with curiosity.

"It's a huge community that has been settled in Toronto since the beginning of the last century," I said, thinking carefully not to give a wrong answer.

Here and there I kept using Serbian words, just for reference, keeping the conversation totally in English.

"How's hunting in Serbia?" I asked him, changing the subject.

"Top notch!" Danillo said and handed me a flyer written in both languages, English and Serbian, as he guided us through the traffic. "During the eighties, hunting was one of the main profitable sources for the Serbian economy." He pointed to a hill in the distance. "There are approximately six thousand different plant species which have been registered on Serbian territory," Danillo said with pride.

"Wow," I said. "That's amazing."

"Exactly right! Serbia is among the leading countries in Europe for the number of wolves. The same goes for the bears."

"Which one is the most significant species to shoot?"

"Of course the Chamois. It costs thousands of euros to shoot one Chamois."

"Where can I shoot a Chamois?"

"You might be able to hunt them in rocky areas. Probably the best place to hunt them is the canyon of the Drina River."

"Is that the top game?"

"No, the red deer is. The hunting season for this kind of game lasts from August to mid-February."

"I guess I am here at the right time and place."

"Yes, you are!" Danillo replied. "Our hunters are proud of the fact that in the second half of the twentieth century the biggest catch of deer in Europe was shot in Serbia, and it was the world champion catch for two full decades."

"Really?"

"Yes!"

"Where are the habitats?"

"Our biggest habitats are in eastern Serbia and the Deliblato Sands, not far from Belgrade. Although sometimes referred to as European deer, unlike the fallow deer that can be found all over the continent, the red deer is very rare in Europe. It is very expensive to shoot them. Foreign hunters also go for roe deer, which live freely in the wild, while Mouflon is only found in fenced hunting reservations. At one time a Mouflon from the Karadjordjevo Reservation was the world champion trophy."

"Very interesting," I said.

"Another valuable kind of game is the wild boar, roaming freely in the wild, as the price of their tusks is sometimes much higher than your Honda, for example." He laughed.

"How do you know that I drive a Honda?" I poked at him.

"I don't, but I once heard that the most sellable cars in Toronto are Honda and Toyota. I ought to mention the small game as well, which is found in abundance in Serbia. The hare population is always well preserved, just like that of partridges, but certainly the special place is reserved for pheasants."

"How many pheasant farms do you guys have?"

"There are more than twenty pheasant farms. The biggest one is the Ristovaca Farm near Bac, where more than three hundred thousand birds are raised every year. It all depends on the preferences of the hunters who come to Serbia year round, but it seems that our country is something of a rare, exotic hunting country in Europe," Danillo said with pride.

We kept talking about hunting in Serbia and it took us more than two hours to get to the hunting ground of Stara Planina II. I could hardly wait to see my real prey, Dragan Spasic. As I started to look around in all directions for any familiar face, I noticed five hunters of the hunting agency "Alfa" coming toward us to give us a special welcome. I looked at each of them, but none of them was Dragan.

The agency boss was a man in his fifties, a big heavy-set man with a very short moustache under his big potato nose. He squeezed my hand like he was trying to amputate it and invited me into the barracks. We all sat around a fancy table made of olivewood, and the big boss from the hunting agency welcomed me and Danillo in broken English. Two other hunters didn't bring guns with them, but the other three had. One of the three brought his gun all the way from Great Britain, the second one from California, USA, and the last hunter who brought a gun with him had come from Germany.

"Welcome from my heart, my dear friends. I am very happy to have you all here tonight. My name is Boris Vucic and I am going to be with you all week long, hunting the most beautiful wild boars on the face of the planet," he said.

As he described the hunting ground of Stara Planina II, I felt a growing excitement anticipating the moment when I would have a gun in my hands. I could feel my heart pounding in my chest and my hair was prickling at the roots. My blood was pulsating through my veins. I couldn't sit still.

Boris Vucic interrupted his short speech and served us hot tea. I drank the tea in one gulp, eager to know what was going to happen next. I didn't have a gun yet and hadn't seen Dragan, the wildest boar in the whole area. Boris seemed to take his time.

"We are going to be together for five days. During this time, we are going to shoot wild boar. Stara Planina is going to be your hotel, one of the best around. We are going to hunt right after midnight, but before we get there, we have to supply guns for our three fellow hunters," he said.

The thought ran through my mind: finally I was going to

have a gun, a real gun, with real bullets that can leave a giant pig weighing one ton without breath.

Boris got up from his chair and pointed to a steel cage where the hunting rifles were kept. He took three guns out and handed them to us. I held mine in my hands and still couldn't believe it. I was so close to my destiny and it was not a dream. I was in Serbia with a gun in my hand and no one was saying anything. Someone was still missing in the big picture: Dragan Spasic!

"This gun is called Fabarm Aspel Double Rifle," said Boris with pride. He picked up a booklet from one of the shelves and read it aloud.

"Here is some technical data on this weapon. The gauge is 30.06-9, 3x 74R. The frame is made of forged steel. As you can see, the barrel length is fifty-five centimetres. Length of pull is 367 millimetres. It weighs 3.25 kilograms and the case is made of aluminium."

Boris Vucic was describing the gun, but my mind was not there. I had been one full day in Serbia and time was ticking away. Based on my research and the news published on Serbian website B92, Dragan's location was right where I was. It didn't really matter that his picture was published under a different identity. Perhaps Alfa had other workers as well. They would have also hired other people. I was impatient to see him. We had to start hunting in a few hours.

After the introduction, we went to our rooms for a break. Stara Planina was a five-star hotel, with a swimming pool indoors, a nice huge TV and beautiful patios. I tried to relax and enjoy it for at least a few minutes. This part of the trip already cost me five Gs. Where was Dragan hiding? My information was probably wrong. I thought for a moment that I was wasting my time here. I closed my eyes and struggled not to give myself a hard time. I had to be fresh and strong for the upcoming meeting.

NINETEEN

Bjeshka e Qershizës hill was clad in an extraordinary green. Five motorcyclists formed a line spaced by ten meters as they rode up the path on the hill. Riding the motorcycles was made more difficult by the fallen trees and the thick shrubbery. After a three-hour ride, the alpinists arrived at the Cave of the Female Bear. Captain "Buja" took his helmet off and wiped the sweat dripping down his forehead. He put two fingers in his mouth and whistled. The motorists gathered around him. Commander Buja pointed to the cave and walked toward it. He entered first, holding a hand light. The dim light showed the wet surface of the cave, which was covered in a thick layer of algae. Several night bats burst out of the deep belly of the cave, flew overhead and scattered off into the forest. The noise surprised the men, but silence settled again once they had gone. They saw stalactites and stalagmites at the entrance of the cave that glittered when the spotlight fell on them. Commander Buja entered deeper into the labyrinth of the cave and found an old suitcase. He lifted the lid carefully and pulled hunting rifles from it. He handed them over to the last alpinists of the group and stepped outside.

TWENTY

The next morning, I showed up in front of the hotel, holding the gun over my shoulder. I caressed it. That sleek piece of weaponry made me feel powerful and confident. Within minutes, the other hunters joined me and all five of us jumped into the four-by-four and drove toward the pine forest.

Boris Vucic and I climbed up a wooden tower that was located beside a swamp covered by various shrubs and trees. Boris pointed to a narrow lane from where the wild boars were supposed to emerge. It was so quiet I could hear a lonely bee buzzing close by. Our truck was parked behind us, on the side of the unpaved road that disappeared off into the woods. Boris handed me the field glasses and climbed down the wooden tower. I followed him down and joined the other three hunters. The agency gave us uniforms similar to those of the Serbian army. I looked like a *chetnik*, a volunteer Serbian militant. Over the military jackets we wore yellow reflective mesh vests in order to be seen in the darkness of night. My boots felt heavy from the mud that clung to them as we made our way through the swamp.

As time passed, we realized we weren't as lucky as we had thought. Boris told us to take a little break before we continued our hunt. We sat on top of a hill. Boris lifted his gun and unloaded it, aiming it into the air.

"Before we hunt for real, I just want to remind you of your own safety. Hunting doesn't end right after you shoot the boar. When the boar is lying there, that doesn't mean that it is dead. You always have to be ready for the unexpected. Make sure you have a cartridge loaded in your gun until you determine that the boar is really dead. You have to be able to protect yourself at all times."

Boris held a single cartridge in the palm of his hand. At that moment I felt the fever of the hunt. In fact, I had become a real hunter.

Hours passed and nothing happened. Three of us climbed the

watch tower again and surveyed the surrounding area, especially the narrow pathways which disappeared into the pine woods. It was a little cold since it was the beginning of September.

Then the very first wild boar appeared. He looked lonely having separated from the herd. It walked between the bushes, unaware that death awaited it.

A loud blast of gunfire echoed. I turned left to see Danillo had pulled the trigger without even realizing it. He had used just one cartridge, but that was enough to hit the boar on its back. It didn't fall right away, but I saw a light cloud of dust rising off its grey hide. Through my field glasses I saw a stream of blood flowing from its wound.

The boar ran toward the bushes, but another bullet hit it in the back. It couldn't keep its balance and fell to the ground. First I saw its back legs fall, then its entire body slid to the ground, shaking for a few minutes till it released its last breath. It stopped moving. I had never seen a wild boar in my life, let alone in the last seconds of its life. Boris' advice came to my mind. I shouldn't run right over to check out the catch. If I did I should at least have the gun loaded, ready to shoot if it was still alive.

Danillo yelled with joy and ran toward the boar without having second thoughts. Right at that minute, twelve boars appeared not far from where we were standing. Boris loaded his gun and shot several times. I did too. It was the first time I was shooting in Serbia and I felt a little emotional. Hunting had become my new thrill, even though it was just a temporary cover.

All five hunters were shooting at them in excitement. The two hunting dogs remained tied to the trees. They barked and pulled at their ropes. Boris untied them one by one, letting them free. The first hunting dog, the one with a big white spot on its forehead, ran toward the dead boar. The second dog ran after Boris as he ran toward the group of boars. I followed him, breathing with difficulty.

I studied the boar lying dead on the forest floor. Boris grabbed a fallen branch which had leaves on it and brushed it in the blood that was still dripping from the open wound on the boar's shoulder. He stuck the branch on Danillo's hat. Danillo's eyes shone with joyful pride. It was a tradition followed by most hunters. Boris grabbed another bunch of leaves and placed them onto the wound.

That was a long night of hunting, and we killed seven boars. I didn't see Dragan Spasic. He was no where to be found. I had only seven days at my disposal and after my time was gone, I would have to leave Serbia without having accomplished my mission.

We tied the dead boars with ropes and threw them on the back of the truck and drove to the Alfa headquarters. I stared at their sharp tusks and struggled with myself to rein in the thrill of the hunt that I was experiencing. I didn't want to sympathize with the way the Serbs were doing business. I didn't want to sympathize with them at all for anything, but deep in my heart I knew I had to learn from them.

After half an hour's drive, we arrived at our camp and stopped the truck beside the tents. Boris went into the wood yard, grabbed a few pieces of firewood and sprayed them with gas. He lit them with a match and tongues of fire engulfed the wood slowly. He took care of everything.

That night we roasted boar on the spit. It was so exciting to see the wild boar roasting, turning around over the fire. I didn't like to eat pork, since I was Muslim, but I had to eat whatever they ate to remain inconspicuous. When Danillo handed me a piece of the pork, which was still steaming hot, I took it without hesitation then chewed it slowly. One small little mistake could spark doubt and questions. It was the first time in my life that I ate the meat of wild boar, and I liked its taste.

When we got back to the cabin, I decided to phone Arben. I found a public phone, checked the area to ensure I was alone and dialed the number.

"Hello, Arben?"

"Hello! How was the trip?"

"So far so good! Are you guys already there?"

"Yes, we are here."

"Look, I got to go. I will call you again," I said and hung up on him. There was no need to talk too long on the phone.

TWENTY-ONE

Boris Vucic didn't show up on the second day of hunting. The Agency Alfa sent Dragan Spasic instead. I recognized him right away, as soon as he came into the main hall of Stara Planina. He looked old and his shoulders drooped. I couldn't see the hate or anger that I remembered from the last time I saw him. He kept silent and wasn't friendly with the other hunters.

"*Doberdan*! My name is Dragan," he said.

He shook my hand and held it tight. It was the same hand that killed my mother and three sisters. I clenched my teeth and shook his hand. My heart was pounding so hard I felt he must feel it through my hand.

Finally, I have you, Dragan Spasic. I spent so many years looking for you. Now is the time you pay for the lives you ruined.

A voice inside me was growing, urging me to grab him by the neck and kill him right on the spot. Another voice, more reasonable, advised me that the time hadn't yet come to kill him.

The second day of hunting was similar to the previous one, but more tense. Every step I took, every move I made, I felt the presence of evil beside me. There were five hunters in our group. That day we were shooting pigeons in a cornfield at a huge farm.

Danillo fired the first shot. I saw the pigeon fall into the field. The hunting dogs ran after it, bringing the prey to the hunter. I held my breath and shot at a pigeon myself. I knew I had to aim a little ahead of the pigeon. When I saw my first pigeon falling from the sky, and looked from the corner of my eye at Dragan, I felt great relief. I was pretty close to him. I had a gun in my hand, but still couldn't do anything. If I shot him right away, I would get caught in a matter of seconds. I had only seven days at my disposal to accomplish my plan to kill him. I was always in a group with the rest of the hunters, and it was very hard to kill someone and not be seen by the others.

On the third day we were hunting wild boar again, and Dragan went deep into the woods. It was one in the early morning and everyone was looking in different directions. I touched the bullets with the tips of my fingers and caressed the thirty-two millimetre hunting gun. I could get rid of him with one shot. I just had to pull the trigger and he would be gone from the face of the planet.

The Serbian hunting ground was pretty close to Presevo city, which was mostly inhabited by Albanians. I lifted my gun and pointed at him in the dark. I could see him, but he couldn't see me. If I killed him, the only thing I had to do was run a few meters and ask for help at any Albanian home in Presevo. The Serbs wouldn't catch me.

Dragan Spasic held a position not far from me. He was pointing at a wild boar that must have weighed over one hundred and twenty kilograms. The boar had black spiky hair and its eyes were red. It quivered and suddenly charged toward Dragan. Dragan lost his footing and the gun fell from his hand. For a moment I didn't understand what was happening. I saw my gun vomiting fire and smoke. The wild boar fell to the ground, wounded. I had hit him twice, once in the head and another on its back.

I had shot the boar twice when I could have shot Dragan! What kind of superpower made me change the direction of my gun? Suddenly weak, my feet couldn't support my body and I almost collapsed. The snout of the fallen boar was inches from my boots. A hand touched my shoulder.

"Hvala vam mnogo. Možete samo spasilo život." ("Thank you very much. You just saved my life.") I turned my head. Dragan made the Sign of the Cross on his chest and hugged me. It was the same man who had killed my sisters and my mother. I couldn't believe it. I had saved his life!

Triumphant, Dragan Spasic screamed at the dead boar. He lifted its head with an evil joy, mocking it. That was the moment when Dragan turned his head toward me and looked straight into my eyes. He dipped his fingers in the blood of the boar and licked them as the other three hunters joined us.

"Da li ste to? On je ubio svinja," ("Did you see that? He killed the boar,") Dragan Spasic said and danced around the dead animal.

I didn't speak. I closed my eyes instead to forget what I had done. My knees felt weak with shame and despair. I knelt and held my head with both hands. With my eyes closed, I saw the image of my mother. She was walking toward me, smiling. She wore a long red dress and her black hair was blowing in the wind. She kissed me on my forehead and then disappeared. I opened my eyes and finally realized that it was an illusion. Perhaps my mother wanted to tell me something very important, but the presence of the other hunters had stopped her. It was my mother, I guessed, who had pushed the gun away at the very last second. Or something worse than that, I feared. I guessed my mother was sending me a message. Her message was that I had to be more careful. The time had not come to kill him yet.

The whole incident reminded me of when I was just a ten-year-old boy and had witnessed helplessly as this man, this murderer, had destroyed our lives.

I got scared, thinking that I might not be able to get the job done. I worried that to do these kinds of things, I had to be a born criminal. Babi had said that to me. I couldn't be just a normal guy and kill, even if the motive to do so was strong. Why had I hesitated? I could finish Dragan for good and that would be the end of my nightmares.

The whole time I remained in the company of the other hunters. If I used my own hunting gun to kill him, it was going to be just a matter of time before I got caught, or in the worst case scenario, killed. I would most likely end up in jail. I stood so close to him with a gun in my hand, but I couldn't safely shoot him just then.

No, it was none of these reasons. I knew I had to ask him some questions before I finished him off. Why did he do it? What kind of explanations would he give me? If he was ever able to explain... If I killed him now, he would not have the chance to clarify why he killed fifteen children and five women in cold blood. Dragan Spasic had to confess in front of me why he did it and show me where the mass grave was. Dragan Spasic had the right to a confession and had to say his own last words to his family, before I sent him to hell.

Dragan waved at me, telling me to come closer. I made up my mind to wait, and walked toward him slowly.

"Congrats, man!" Danillo patted me on the shoulder.

The boar was heavy and we struggled to lift it with ropes. We dumped it on the back of the truck and drove to the camp.

Dragan kept talking excitedly about the boar that I had killed as it attacked him. His eyes were shining in the dark. When we arrived at the camp, Dragan did the same thing that Boris did the previous night. He went to the wood yard and picked a few pieces of firewood. We sat for a few hours around a big fire, eating pieces of roast meat and drinking *Slivovica*.

On the fourth night of hunting, it was me and Dragan alone and no one else. The night was beautiful and the sky was filled with stars. I could hear the light chirping of the grasshoppers. I was holding the gun in my hands and feeling the adrenaline rush through me. The pickup truck was parked beside the pathway.

"I want you to come and visit my home. I want to introduce you to my family," Dragan said, catching me by surprise. "It is going to be like a big thank-you to you for saving my life," he said and laughed. I could see real joy in his eyes. He was serious and didn't have a clue who I was.

I had never thought that he would make such a request! I felt an ache in my heart when I thought of Slavica and Nenad. Were they living with their father? She was probably around twenty-six years old and Nenad my age, around twenty-five. I wondered what they looked like.

"Whereabouts do you live?" I asked him, trying to avoid eye contact. I didn't want him to see what I was feeling at that moment.

"I live in Belgrade with my wife. I have a son and a daughter who live in Belgrade as well. They are both married, but I can call them over and have a big party. What do you think?" he insisted.

"I don't know what to say. It would be nice! Let me think about it," I said and walked through the bushes.

There was no way that I would drive back to Belgrade in his company. I could never kill him in front of Nenad, or even worse, in front of Slavica. I would get caught in a few minutes. Even if I escaped, the whole Belgrade police force would be after me. *Why do I have to complicate things when it is so convenient to do it right now? I am here in the middle of nowhere. If I kill him, she won't even know why her father was killed.*

Am I really a killer? Was I born a killer? Why do I have to be a killer like him? How can I hide a killing for the rest of my life? A fake passport can't hide a killing for too long. What if I take him hostage and bring him in front of a court in Kosovo instead? Interpol couldn't find him, but I was able to do it. What am I really looking for? I am not looking for revenge. I am looking for justice. There is a big difference between revenge and justice.

I stopped pretending that I was looking for the boar and pointed the gun at him. I could see his face change in surprise.

"What are you doing?" he whispered with a weak voice.

"Get in the car!" I said, and pulled the trigger a little. "Do you remember me?"

"Bogdan!"

"I am not Bogdan, you dumbass!"

"Then who are you?" Dragan was beginning to panic.

"My name is Ermal Bllaca. I'm an Albanian!"

"An Albanian? That's impossible," he cried out.

"You better believe it," I said firmly and closed in on him.

I took out one of my contact lenses, always pointing the gun at him. My eyes were one brown, one blue. He could see that I wasn't Bogdan. He walked backward and fell to the ground, but got up again quickly.

"What do you want from me?" His voice was shaking.

I took one more step toward him. "I was a ten-year-old boy when I saw you killing my mother and three little sisters."

Dragan tried to move his hand down to his waist, but I pointed the gun once again to his head, moving even closer.

"I don't remember you. I think you've got the wrong person."

"It happened on April 3rd, 1999, in Gjakova, Kosovo. You came with four other policemen, and killed twenty women and children. We were in the basement. The guy who pulled the trigger was the same height as you. You have the same blue eyes as him. You have the same birthmark under your neck."

"I don't know what you're talking about. I am telling you, you've got the wrong guy."

"Shut up! Look at your right arm. You have the tattoo, a tiger on your right arm. Your nose is bumpy, the same as his."

Dragan's face darkened. He didn't speak. In one-tenth of a second, he put his right hand on his gun. My foot shot out and I kicked his gun away and placed the barrel of my gun to his forehead.

"Keep your hands up!" I screamed at him. Dragan let the gun lie on the ground. "It's payback time. But before you go straight to hell, I need you to tell me why you did it. Why did you?"

Dragan kept silent. His lower lip quivered. I saw tears in his eyes. I couldn't believe that one of the most notorious Death Squad members would appear so weak.

"They were not soldiers. They didn't have any guns. Why did you kill them?"

Dragan tried to articulate something then spluttered, "We had orders!"

"What orders? From who?"

"We had an order to kick all the Albanians out from Kosovo." His face became drawn with fear. He started to walk backward as I came closer to him. I kicked his gun aside. I grabbed his arms and tied his hands behind his back. I pushed him toward the pickup truck.

"Please, don't kill me! Please!" he begged in a broken voice. "Where are we going?" he asked again as he got in the truck. I slammed the door shut and started the engine. It was going to be a very short drive to Kosovo. The border was only half an hour's drive away.

"You are going in front of a EULEX court in Kosovo," I said, ready to put the handbrake off and the gear in drive position.

"Not yet!" I heard someone shout, and a single shot went straight to the left back tire. Another bullet hit the windshield. I bent down on the front seat as much as I could and covered my face as glass shattered all around me. For more than a minute, I just kept hiding behind the wheel, trying to escape the bullets aimed at me. Finally, I realized I had to do something. I pressed the gas pedal and checked the direction ahead. It was a very narrow path, not paved, covered here and there by thorns and bushes. Huge branches of trees were in my way. As I was struggling to hold on, keeping both hands on the wheel, the pickup truck spun out of control and hit a tree. A cloud of smoke came out from the engine as the spray of bullets kept flying around the truck. I feared that the truck could catch on fire at any moment.

The shooting stopped. I heard the same wild and thick voice behind, this time behind my ear.

"Get the hell out of the truck and keep your hands up!"

I couldn't believe my ears. Even the grasshoppers stopped their light chirping. I lifted my hands up in despair, looking at the sky with sorrow. The stars were dense and brighter as I stepped outside from the truck. The horn blew. I looked back and noticed Danillo's face to my surprise. I had no clue how it could be that he appeared there, where I didn't need him. It was supposed to be a hunting night just for two wild boar hunters, Dragan and me. Danillo stood only two meters away, breathing heavily, holding his rifle with both hands and pointing it right in the middle of my forehead. I felt angry and really disappointed at myself, but there was nothing I could do. In the corner of my eye I caught sight of Dragan Spasic. He struggled out from the back seat, with hands still bound, and approached me with a sneer.

"Now lie down on the ground and put your hands behind your back," Danillo yelled at me. He yelled so loud it hurt my ears.

I lay on the ground and felt the dew on my shivering skin, waiting with my eyes wide open, wondering what would happen next. I listened to my hard breathing, struggling to think of a way out of that situation. I'd been so close to fulfilling my mission and at the very last second I had failed terribly. Despair and anger made my body shiver from head to toe. My clasped fingers were shaking. I hated myself! I hated myself! I hated myself and bit my lower lip, not to give them the pleasure of hearing my agonizing scream. My face was scratched all over by the flying glass from the windshield. My back hurt.

My father's words came into my mind. What did Babi say? The least that could happen to me if I failed was that I would end up in a cell somewhere, where nobody would know where I was and I would never come back alive, and my bones would rot in an unmarked grave. I should try to escape instead of enduring jail time in a Serbian prison.

"Untie me," Dragan yelled at Danillo and in the meantime

kicked my lower ribs with the tip of his shoe. He didn't wait for the rope to be taken off, just kept kicking me harder like a soccer ball, wherever he could: on my feet, on my stomach, on my back, even my head.

My view darkened as I bit my lower lip, trying not to scream. I didn't want to give him the pleasure of seeing me in pain. Despite that, I was aware of the new reality, ending like a boar myself, a tied and wounded boar, unable to protect itself. I heard Dragan's steps going around me. He used the same rope to bind my hands and tightened them really hard, so hard that they dug into my flesh. Dragan Spasic bent over me and grabbed my hair and pulled it, turning my head toward him so quickly I thought he was going to break my neck. I felt so much pain in my neck and imagined this could be the end for me. If the time had come for me to die, let it be that way, but I was not going to scream, to give him any satisfaction. I glared at him with hate and anger.

"*Shiptari*!" Dragan snarled, staring at me with open hatred. "How did you find out where I was? Who sent you here? Interpol? CIA? Talk to me!" he yelled into my ear. He didn't wait for my answer. He kicked my chin. I thought my skull cracked as I felt my head falling, but Dragan didn't stop. He kept kicking me with both feet and shouting aloud in Serbian.

"Are you sure you're an Albanian? You're probably a fucking American! A fucking CIA! What's this? Is this just a joke? You were too good to be an Albanian. You even saved my life back there! Hmm? Why did you do that? Tell me!"

"OK, that's enough!" Danillo pulled him back, still pointing his rifle at my head.

TWENTY-TWO

When I regained consciousness I was tied to a tree. I had no idea how long I had been held hostage, but I noticed that it was still dark, probably a couple more hours until dawn. My left eye was swollen and my throat was dry from thirst. Cold water seeped into my clothes. Dragan Spasic had thrown a bucket of water on me and was smoking a cigar, waiting for me to come back to life. Danillo was blowing the horn, signaling the rest of the hunters to gather where we were. After all those kicks on my head and body, I was not quite sure what brought me back to consciousness. Perhaps the ice water that Dragan dumped on me, or the cool breeze of the early morning, or the sound of the horn blowing.

A carriage pulled by two big black horses brought the rest of the group to the tree to which I was tied. I noticed Boris Vucic from Alfa getting off the carriage. He approached, stopping a few meters from me, and surveyed me, showing surprise. He drilled Dragan with questions in Serbian. They spoke too fast for me to understand. He pointed the flashlight straight on my face, looking for an answer. I closed my eyes instinctively and waited in the dark for the worst to come. I caught a few words: "police," "Interpol," "*shqiptari*." Dragan was dealing with Boris, communicating with him with hands and feet, almost shouting at him with anger. I didn't have even a little hope that Boris would intervene to save me from the iron clutches of Dragan Spasic. They all belonged to the same Serbian faction who hated Albanians.

Boris turned to me. "Why did you do this? Who sent you here? Tell me, if you want to go back to Canada," he warned.

I kept my mouth shut and prepared to die. At any moment I could get the same bullet as the boars, right here in the middle of nowhere. I didn't feel sorry for myself. I just felt a deep regret that I was not able to bring justice to my family.

Boris gave up on me and turned to Dragan. "We hand him over to our police. They can do anything they want with him."

But Dragan vehemently disagreed. He wanted to execute me right there.

"I am going to play a death game with him," Dragan said, sneering. "Like Tom and Jerry. I liked that cartoon movie since I was a child. I am going to bring back my memories from that time. We let him get lost for ten minutes, and after..."

"What? Are you out of your mind?"

"We let him go and count ten minutes, then we chase him. If he escapes our game, he will be a free man again. How's that?" Dragan looked to the other hunters for approval. They erupted in cheers.

"We better hand him over to police," Boris insisted. "They can deal with him!"

Dragan pointed the gun at Boris Vucic this time. He touched the barrel to Boris' forehead and grabbed him by the collar of his jacket.

"Forget the police! He is going to be a boar himself! Then we will shoot him!"

"This is illegal! You can't do that! We are not in a war anymore!"

"Yes we are, until the end! If it wasn't for Danillo, I would be dead by now."

"He didn't have the intention to kill you! He could have done that before, but he saved your life instead!"

"Shut up! Do what I say, or you can leave if you wish!"

"Okay, I'll leave!" Boris stepped backward, looking doubtfully at Dragan. He lifted his hands up instinctively, then turned and walked into the woods.

The rest of the hunters waited, wondering what would happen next. Dragan sniffed angrily and rubbed his chin thoughtfully. He bent to face me directly. Several seconds passed. I could feel his hard breath on my face. Then he reached over and unbound my hands and grabbed my arm, pulling me to get up. I struggled to my feet, steeling my strength to manage my bruised body and weakened knees. The only chance I had for life was the death game that Dragan was pushing me to play.

"It's your turn now!" He turned back on me angrily. "You are free to go!" I froze in front of him. I was in a dilemma. If I started running, he could shoot me right on the spot. I stood frozen in indecision. "I said go! Did you hear me?" he yelled.

My feet moved a little. I felt so much pain. I just wanted to lay on the ground and sleep. Sleep indeed! His voice echoed in my ears! I had to go. I had to go... I had...

I took the first step backward, looking at Dragan. The wind coming from the forest brought to my nose the smell of freedom. Dried leaves crackled under my feet. Even though I was physically wounded, I felt I could become a free man once again.

I ran into the forest.

I felt a supernatural energy take over my body. To run faster, I had to breathe with my mouth open. The cold air was a snake bite to my lungs. I didn't have time to think. I had to run as fast as I could, zigzagging in order to avoid bullets.

Behind me I heard Dragan laughing sarcastically and after a few seconds a bullet whistled by close to my ear. I felt something trickling down my left cheek. I wiped my hand across it and saw blood. The bullet had grazed me slightly. I found the strength to keep going. I fell to the ground and crawled forward carefully and hid behind a tree. I waited and waited... and waited. There was no sign that the rest of the hunters were approaching.

As I prepared to run again, something—an animal? —leapt at me from behind the tree. I almost screamed, then a warm hand covered my mouth and I felt relief as I recognized the voice in my ear.

"Shsht! It's me, Arben!" he said in a hoarse whisper. The man removed his hand from my mouth and took off his black hood. I couldn't speak, just stared at him. Even though many years had passed, I recognized him right away. His hair had thinned a little, but the warm look in his eyes had not changed.

"How did you come up here?" I asked him.

"We don't have time to talk about it now," he said shortly and whistled. A shadow emerged from a bush, holding a hunting rifle in his left hand, and approached us cautiously. I glanced at Arben and saw him smile. The man took his hood off and lifted his arms to hug me. My heart pounded so hard, I thought it would come out of my chest. It was my father.

"Babi!"

He put a finger on his lips, giving me a signal to keep quiet. The hunters could be heard coming close to where we were hiding, but passed us by. We lay on the ground for a while, until we couldn't hear their voices anymore. When I felt it was safe enough to get up, I rose to my feet and hugged my father. As I was holding him tight in my arms, I felt his body shivering with an inner sobbing.

We started to walk away slowly into the dark forest, trying to leave the danger behind. We were deep into the territory of Serbia and could get caught either by Serbian army or police patrols.

It was almost dawn when we entered Kosovo and all three of us were exhausted.

Looking at the dark sky, as if for the first time in fifteen years, I saw my mother coming toward me. She hugged me and held me tight in her arms. I was once again the same little boy who escaped alive when her dead body covered me as she fell.

The next day we went to Prishtina Airport and took a flight to Canada. When we arrived home, coming by bus from Pearson Airport, I felt like I had never left. Nothing had changed in the metropolitan city of Toronto. Nothing had changed in my home. But I knew: I had changed forever. I was not the man buried in the past as before. At least I had tried to get justice for my family.

PART THREE

THE THIN LINE

TWENTY-THREE

My emotions were coiled like a spring in my chest. As the days passed, Babi went back to his routine. But it was different for me. The anger and the disappointment gnawed at me. I'd lost my head when I was so close to success. I spent days analyzing in detail what really happened. We had to start everything from the beginning all over again, but with one big disadvantage: Dragan Spasic and his friends were aware of the relatives of the victims looking for them. Just a few days ago, Dragan was unaware of the danger and enjoyed himself hunting boar. I would not be so easy to go to Serbia and grab him by the throat.

I started to have nightmares again. I didn't sleep well and the future seemed totally dark. Babi noticed how disturbed I was, but he pretended he didn't see anything and kept his routine of waking up early morning for work; coming back in the evening exhausted; going straight to the shower; having dinner; and paying a short visit to his lady friend Vjollca.

I continued to look up Dragan Spasic on Google and other search engines. Sometimes searching for the names of Blago Stojkovic and Nemanja Djuric. But I couldn't find anything worthwhile on the internet. Then news about the Bytyqi Brothers caught my attention. They had joined the Atlantic battalion in 1999, but they were caught by the Serbian army and taken to jail, where they were executed. It was their fourth brother, an American citizen who pushed the case forward and increased the pressure on the US government to ask Serbia to bring the perpetrators to justice. Their case made me optimistic that I was not the only one who was looking for war criminals. The man who gave the order for their execution was nicknamed "Guri." He was the right hand of the current prime minister of Serbia and was elected a member of parliament in Serbia. The Bytyqi Brothers' case was a sensitive issue between the US and Serbian governments.

As I read about the case, I concluded that my own plan had one huge flaw that had caused me to fail. I had worked independently and alone to get to Dragan and the other Gjakova killers. I should start coordinating with institutions in Kosovo, at least to get information. My only contact with the Kosovo Intelligence Agency was Arben Morina, who had a direct interest in finding the mass grave of the Gjakova victims. There was no way I would give up. I didn't even think about that. The search and recovery plan was halfway through and there was no way of going back to the starting point. It didn't matter that I had failed once.

I kept gathering information about all three of my targets. Dragan, Blago and Nemanja were among the few people who knew the location of the mass grave. If I found just one of them, then there was a very good chance of finding the remains of our dead. Were they still in Serbia, or did they go overseas and change their identities? I watched the daily news on the main channels and read all the main newspapers online, copying and pasting any news about Serbian war criminals who were being tracked in Europe and elsewhere. I printed the news clips and made a file. Even if they didn't seem related to my case, I reread them carefully, trying to pay attention to all the small details. If they were still hiding in Serbia, who was going to get them? Could I still get in with a different identity, the same way I had done before?

The nightmares continued. My mother's ghost appeared everywhere I went. The graves of my family were still empty. I started to hear their voices whispering in my ears those words I did not want to hear.

Give it up! You don't have to worry about us anymore! You tried to do your best, but it didn't work. What else can you do? There is nothing for you to be ashamed of. You survived once, when you went over the edge. The Lord and chance saved you twice. Life cannot be spared three times. The third time is going to be the real time.

I woke up with fear in the middle of the night, but there was nobody around. The voices of the dead came back to me in my imagination. I plugged my ears with my fingers, but their voices came through, going through my mind, begging me to give up. They came into me through my breath, through the pores of my skin. I clenched my fists and made up my mind not to fail in my mission. There was no way I would stop searching for Dragan and others. But perhaps I could step back a little, following the events from a distance, waiting for them to commit just one little mistake.

I started working as a cabinet-maker, the same profession as my father's. I worked forty hours per week and the rest of the time I spent collecting information. I called Arben every weekend, but there was nothing new as usual. I was brainstorming all the time, putting myself in Dragan's shoes, asking where would I hide, and I surprised myself with my answer. I could hide in the Greek part of Cyprus Island or perhaps in downtown Toronto, just a few meters away from where I lived. Perhaps...

Almost five months had passed and I found myself deep into the daily monotony: work-home, homework, but never forgetting my internet surfing for hours, until my eyelids became heavy. I knew it seemed crazy to search that way, but I still tried to search on Google for all the three names on my short 'List,' one by one. There were over ninety-six thousand results for the name of Dragan Spasic. Some photos of different people with the same name and last name, but none of the photos belonged to the Dragan Spasic that I knew. I found only one photo of him a few months ago, but it had since been deleted. He must be keeping a low profile, I figured, sensing that I would not give up on him.

I touched the keyboard with the tips of my fingers and searched for a different name, Blago Stojkovic, who was the second name on the List. Within thirty-seven seconds I was able to find eighty-five thousand hits, but none of them had to do with the group of the Jackals. As I was almost ready to shut down the computer, I tried the third name on the List, Nemanja Djuric. And bang! A burst of emotion went through my body like a high voltage current. There were one hundred and sixty thousand results within seconds, but just one result gave me the green light of a "direct hit." There was only one Nemanja Djuric who had his right leg amputated and replaced with an artificial one. It was a recent news item about Nemanja Djuric, who was caught in Bosnia by the SAS and NAVY SEALs and was taken to a high security prison in Wakefield in the United Kingdom. He was the only person that I had identified so far from that close circle of people who knew about the whereabouts of the mass grave where my relatives were buried.

I printed the news published in the British newspaper *Daily Mail*, which was about the arrest of Nemanja Djuric and his isolation in the notorious Wakefield prison. Her Majesty's Prison Wakefield was a Category A men's prison located in Wakefield, West Yorkshire, England. I was thinking of how to get to that man in a high security prison when I heard a signal from Skype. I always left the Skype app on so I could hear the click on my cell wherever I was.

Arben Morina had heard the news too.

"Did you know about the news? 'The Handicap' went to jail," Arben whispered, as if he was afraid that someone was listening to him.

"How can we get in touch with 'The Handicap'? I am afraid that our chances to get some info from him are zero."

"There's a one percent chance! There's an Albanian prisoner in there who can ask 'The Handicap' where the mass grave is."

"Who is this guy?"

"Lirim Berisha from Drenica, Kosovo. He was charged with first-degree murder and got life in prison. He started to spend his time behind bars last year and was transferred to Wakefield six months ago. Here, I got the address of the Wakefield prison. It's on 5 Love Lane, five minutes' walk from a local subway station."

"How can we contact this man?" I asked him again, rising in my chair.

"Check the website of the United Kingdom's Ministry of Justice. I am sending the link to you right now! You see that?"

"Yeah, I see it!"

"Someone might contact a prisoner only if the prisoner agrees. Here's the deal: why don't you try to send him an e-mail directly? Write to him that you are from the same region of Drenica and that his father Ibrahim asked you to see him in jail and find out how he is doing."

"Did you speak to his father?" I asked him.

"I was at his home last night. His father Ibrahim was so happy, he couldn't believe that someone would pay a visit to his son in jail. He thought it's quite impossible."

"Did you explain to him why we have to visit his son in prison?"

"Of course! I told him straight. 'We want to find the remains of our relatives who were killed at Milosh Gilica Street. There is a Serbian inmate at the same prison who might know about it and we want your son to contact him directly.' That's all I said to him and he totally agreed."

"Do you think it's possible to pay this visit to him in prison? Don't the prison staff check the e-mails?"

"All the e-mails go through them. You can check the web for your personal knowledge. There's a map of the location, all the rules that a visitor has to follow, everything you might need," he said.

I began to feel hopeful listening to his voice, which was full of hope and confidence. I felt relieved, but I was still undecided.

"Since it's that easy, I can send him an e-mail tonight," I said. "It might be a possibility that he might not reply back. What do we have to do in that case?"

"He will be happy that someone wants to see him, for sure. Write to him 'salut' from his own father Ibrahim from Drenica. That will do it."

"Don't the prison staff record the conversation?"

"Speak to him in Albanian, but backward. It was a game Lirim practiced when he was a teenager."

"All right! There is nothing to lose anyway," I said excitedly, and felt the adrenaline rush in my veins. I guessed I was in good position, since Lirim's father had given his approval for me to contact his son in jail.

I got off Skype and searched on the internet for the Wakefield prison. There I found a link to the Ministry of Justice of the United Kingdom and started my virtual tour inside the shadowy Wakefield walls. I wanted to make sure that a relative or a close friend could visit the Albanian gangster Lirim Berisha, who was spending life in prison for a beating in a night club which resulted in the loss of life of a Pakistani national, a father of two kids. There I found an interesting page for an "email a prisoner service." I clicked on www.emailaprisoner.com, and for only thirty-five pounds I was able to send a message directly to Lirim Berisha. The message was going to be read by the prison staff first, then it was going to be sent by the prison officials to the prisoner in hand. I signed myself up and started to write it.

"To whom it may concern! My name is Ermal Bllaca, an Albanian from Kosovo, living in Toronto, Canada. I am writing on behalf of Ibrahim Berisha, father of Lirim Berisha, who is a prisoner in the Wakefield prison. His father Ibrahim wants me to pay a visit to his son. I am asking for Lirim's permission so I can come and visit him... Thank you in advance."

I clicked "Send" and another page appeared on the screen. I paid thirty-five pounds via PayPal and waited. My view turned foggy as I kept straining at the computer screen. I was shivering, but waited for a few hours. There was no immediate answer, so I waited one full day, then two days.

After two sleepless days I finally got a reply. The prisoner Lirim Berisha had accepted my visit in the glassy cell of Monster Manson. But my job was not done. I had to call the number 01924 to book a legal visit. Legal visit telephone booking times were Monday to Friday from nine am to eleven-thirty am, Tuesday, Wednesday and Thursday two pm to four pm.

My next concern was how to get to the UK. After my arrival at Heathrow airport, I had to take a train to the nearest mainline station of Wakefield Westgate, and the prison was about a five-minute walk away.

* * *

Lirim Berisha was around thirty, tall, and with blue eyes. He had shaved his hair. He was handcuffed. Before we sat at the table, I was aware of the fact that there was a microphone installed on the table and the whole conversation was going to be recorded and checked later by the prison staff. I noticed two prison guards watching the whole visitor's area through a glass wall. As soon as I saw him coming, I recognized him from the photo Arben sent me via email, even though I had never seen him before. The photo was taken when Lirim was a teenager.

He hadn't changed much; only his eyes had lost their innocence. He came straight to the table where I was sitting. I guessed that he recognized me too, even though he'd never met me before in his life. The prison guard probably gave him instructions on which table to go to. I waved at him and stood up anxiously, but his stony expression didn't change. I had only ten minutes for my visit and had to speak clearly to him, making sure he would understand what I wanted from him.

"Si jeni?" ("How are you?") I asked him gently in Albanian, finding a way to start the conversation. He shook his head in displeasure, making me understand that "you know how it is" and stared at me directly, as if he was trying to drill through me.

"A e teyp nitakas es uk naj et tirukedv?" ("Can you ask 'the Handicap' where are the dead?") I asked him in Albanian, but this time saying the Albanian words backward, letter by letter. Lirimi's face darkened. For one moment he betrayed confusion. It took a minute or so, until he realized in what language code I was speaking to him. I noticed a light smile at the corner of his mouth. He shook his head in approval.

"Et fosh...!" ("Let me see...!") He spoke Albanian backward. He got up and turned his back. The conversation had lasted less than a minute and it was over. I glanced around the room for any reaction by the prison guards. At the other tables the visits were taking place normally. I sighed, feeling relieved, but still not comfortable deep in my soul.

Now that the visit was over I was back on the road to Canada. I took the train at Wakefield Westgate and traveled back to London, where I got a taxi to Heathrow airport.

TWENTY-FOUR

Nemanja Djuric unhinged his artificial leg and laid it on the bed, which was clean and neat. The cell looked like a matchbox, where everything was placed in order. An orange shirt and pants were folded carefully on a shelf. A small TV set was installed above a cabinet. He felt exhausted and lay on the bed with his face on the pillow. He was tall and his foot stuck out over the edge of the bed. Not more than two weeks had passed in Wakefield prison, but those fourteen days in jail had destroyed him already.

He still couldn't understand how he fell into the trap laid for him. The British Special Forces SAS and US NAVY SEALs had trapped him as he was on the back seat of a four-wheel military jeep driving through the territory of the Republic of Srbska in Bosnia. That particular military area was under the control of a Russian contingent of SFOR, and his arrest was conducted without the knowledge of the Russian command. There was a diplomatic outcry from Serbia and Russia against his detention, but Interpol went ahead with its operation to handcuff Nemanja Djuric and hold him responsible for the war crimes he had committed in Bosnia and Kosovo.

Nemanja Djuric shut his eyelids tight, trying to forget that moment when the tires of the vehicle he was in were drilled through by the spikes laid out on the highway, which forced the driver to fight to control the vehicle. As soon as the jeep braked to a violent stop, the British and US marines appeared on both sides of the road, firing in the air. Two marines broke the side windows and pulled him out like a scared rabbit. Nemanja Djuric fought back, throwing punches and kicks left and right, but a sudden punch on the chin quietened him. He ended up in the so-called "Monster Mansion," side by side with the most dangerous killers on the face of the planet.

He struggled to forget everything, but closing his eyes didn't work. He sat on the bed and looked at the window sill. All of a sudden he noticed some pigeon droppings on the window sill and grimaced. The pigeon droppings were enormous. Since he had a lot of time on his hands, he found it amusing to count them. One, two, three, fifteen, eighteen droppings... Some of the droppings had fallen recently and some were old. An evil feeling swept him from head to toe. He clenched his teeth so hard he felt the pain deep in his gums. That was disgusting for him. He was definitely going to complain to the prison staff about the pigeon droppings on his window sill. Not just for the embarrassment, but the droppings would bring a horde of flies, mosquitoes and other dirty insects to the window. He wanted that piece of blue sky to be a clean view. It was the only view he had. That slice of sky gave him hope and made him alive again.

He took the remote control and turned the TV on. A foggy view appeared on the screen. He shut it off immediately, feeling nervous about it, and sat back on the bed. He was going to complain about the TV as well, that was for sure! Who were they joking with? With a soldier of Serbia, who drove hundreds of people out like flocks of sheep! They didn't really know who they were dealing with, did they? He hit the wall with his fist in an attempt to smash it down. He hit it so hard his knuckles bled.

"Ah," he yelled aloud, but he gave up at the end. He lay back on the bed and tried to forget where he was. Almost an hour had passed, when his eyelids were becoming really heavy and the exhaustion penetrated his bones.

In spring of 1999, a convoy of trucks stopped in the middle of the highway. They were heading to the Serbian capital Belgrade. One of the trucks couldn't handle its heavy load and its doors had burst wide open. Several dead bodies fell on the pavement. The vehicles stopped and the six drivers, helpers, and policemen who were escorting them helped to collect the bodies and load them back on the truck. After several hours' drive, they finally arrived at their destination. The six huge trucks entered the military base of the Yugoslav Army SAJ in the region of XXX. Every one of them had a special load that night: the bodies of the Albanian civilians killed in Kosovo. The soldiers worked all night long to open a row of eight mass graves. It was a very dark night and not even a single star shone in the sky. But there was some sense of fear in the ranks of the Serbian soldiers and policemen; they worried that they would be sighted by the NATO spy airplanes.

As head of the operation, Nemanja Djuric radioed the Ministry of Interior, telling them the truth about the high level of risk of the special operation that they were conducting. The order from above arrived promptly. The Ministry of Defense ordered them to create an artificial shield with smoke, produced by burning car tires. A thick layer of smoke formed in a matter of minutes. It was enough to cover the whole operation. That night over a hundred tires were set ablaze.

The trucks were parked in the military base for more than two weeks. Pretty soon a heavy smell started to spread through the area; it was the stench of rotting flesh. A kind of liquid appeared, dropping from the trucks, a mix of blood and remains and dirt. Some of the soldiers spread toilet-cleaning acid to get rid of the stench, but it was impossible. After the acid didn't have any effect, some of his colleagues spilled gasoline around the parking area where the trucks were loaded and then set the soil on fire.

In his cell, Nemanja Djuric coughed heavily, remembering that the smoke that came from the burning tires had penetrated deep into his lungs. Nemanja had another big problem: there was a fellow prisoner who stared at him whenever he had to go to the prison workshop. The warehouse was a restricted area, where the prisoners spent their free time and practiced their new professions with the hope that one day they would come out of jail and find a suitable place in society.

After a few days he noticed the same prisoner who kept torturing him by just staring fixedly at him was sharpening a teaspoon on the grindstone. It was Lirim Berisha, who had turned his back carefully on his jail instructor and after he made sure that nobody was watching him, kept sharpening the spoon. In the ongoing noise in the warehouse from the plumber wannabes, electricians, welders, builders, sharpening a spoon by a prisoner didn't attract too much attention, except for the fox eyes of Nemanja Djuric.

The teaching instructor placed his personal tools in a safe steel case after making sure that all the screwdrivers, the hammers, the nails, the knives were accounted for, and locked the box carefully. There was nothing missing in the inventory, not even a hammer, a sharp shovel, a pair of pliers, or a pair of scissors. Except for a spoon which was sharpened as a knife by Lirim Berisha, who kept looking left and right, making sure that nobody noticed him.

Lirim stuck his sharpened spoon up his sleeve and stood behind Nemanja, who had watched him since the first moment. Nemanja almost peed his pants from fear, but managed to wait for one of the guards to open the warehouse's door. Lirim turned back to his cell, hoping for another chance to approach Nemanja. The other chance would come very soon, since the prisoners were taking lessons on how to improve their skills in the warehouse three times a week. Most of the prisoners preferred to get in the trade field either as a plumber, a mechanic, a welder or an electrician. Even though he didn't really believe that one day he would be released, Nemanja chose to become a plumber.

As soon as he entered the workshop, he felt the same drilling eyes of Lirim, who had sharpened his spoon just a couple of days ago. He stepped along, making quite sure that he stood a fair distance from him, but Lirim kept following him inside the hall slowly but surely, giving Nemanja the impression that he was getting ready to say something to him, something very important, without the fellow prisoners or the prison guards overhearing him. He seemed to be making up his mind, since he kept changing his expression every time he came toward him and stepped closer. Nemanja could read his face well: the Albanian prisoner wanted to cut his flesh open with the improvised knife, probably right under his short, white-skinned neck.

Nemanja sighed, trying to calm down a little, guessing that Lirim was sharpening the spoon just for protection, nothing to do with him. Once the same prisoner saluted him angrily, without moving even a single muscle of his tense face.

"Hey." He spoke for the first time to him, but Nemanja ignored him, pretending that he was paying attention to the plumbing instructor. After a few minutes, he couldn't resist the urge of fear and curiosity to know who the guy was, so he looked at him straight in the eyes. The young man was around twenty-five, with average height. He noticed a strange fire of hate deep in his brown eyes.

"Hey," Nemanja said back and filed out with the rest of the

prisoners. He had the impression that he had seen that face before. He had similar features of a Balkan-born man. What if he was a Bosnian Muslim or a Croat, or even worse, a Kosovo Albanian? Lirim was touching something with the tips of his fingers, something that was hidden in his waistband. The man pulled out a sharp knife. Nemanja noticed that the knife still had the shape of a spoon, but was much sharper and tied with a spring to the handle of a toothbrush. It was too late to realize that the sharp edge of the spoon-knife had cut him gently in the area of his spleen. Lirim leaned in, pressing the knife deeper, and glared at him.

"Where are the victims from Djakovica buried?" he demanded of Nemanja. "Tell me the place of the mass grave and I promise that I will leave you alone," the prisoner snarled in Serbo-Croatian.

Nemanja noticed a light accent. He wasn't a Slav. He shook with fear, as if he was having a fit. Nemanja pushed him away, but the prisoner grabbed him by the wrist and pulled him closer. Nemanja glanced around for help, but in vain. The prisoner pressed the knife harder. He saw a drop of blood on the floor. Nemanja clenched his teeth in despair, his face all reddened by the nightmare he was experiencing.

I have to do something to escape his clutches. I have to gain some time. Just a little time, then I'll be just fine. He can't scare me! No one can scare a Serbian Jackal!

"What the hell are you talking about?" he shouted at him, keeping his eyes wide open. Lirim didn't like Nemanja's reaction and pulled him tight as Nemanja struggled to escape.

Nemanja took one step backward. Another step backward, feeling safer and triumphant. He would never show him where the mass grave was. The dead couldn't speak, but their bodies were solid proof. There could still be clues, hidden answers that survived the years, if someone was interested to look for justice. Even dead, they could still be evidence before a tribunal. It's hard to punish the killers if there is no proof of victims to be found.

The other leaned into him. "Where did you bury the Albanians from Milos Gilica Street? Talk to me, if you want to stay alive!" Lirim pressed on. This time Nemanja felt a sharp object cutting his neck. He felt a strong pain, and his feet couldn't handle the weight of his body and his view darkened. His artificial limb stood still taking the weight of his body.

"Only the captain knows. He lives in Perth, Western Australia, under the name of Daniel Krieger," he mumbled, feeling himself fall.

"Good boy!" Lirim said, chuckling.

One of the instructors rang the alarm bell. Three prison guards entered the workshop, holding rubber batons in their hands. They noticed that Nemanja lay bleeding on the floor and jumped on Lirim, who was still holding his spoon-knife in his hand, and hit him with batons.

TWENTY-FIVE

The only message that I got from the prisoner Lirim Berisha was a photo cut out of a book of the city of Perth in Western Australia. The photo had only the name "Daniel Krieger" written on it. I couldn't understand what the name Daniel Krieger had to do with anything. I forwarded the photo by Gmail to Arben Morina and turned Skype on, waiting impatiently for him to answer. I frowned, as I was puzzling over the meaning of Lirim's sending a photo from the city of Perth in Western Australia. The name of "Daniel Krieger" didn't ring any bells for me.

Arben came on Skype right away, but this time with a big smile on his face. He seemed to be sure about the reason why Lirim sent that photo to me.

"Did you realize why he sent you that photo? I guess not; that's why you're calling me," he said with an ironic smile.

"I have no clue at all."

"Daniel Krieger might be a nickname for Dragan Spasic."

"It might, but it might not be as well!" I answered sharply. That was my very first guess too, but I would not think that Captain Dragan would be so stupid to leave Serbia and be on the loose right in an English-speaking country like Australia and live there under the name of Daniel Krieger. Most of the war criminals who were declared wanted by Interpol with a summons from The Hague Tribunal were hiding in Serbia, mostly in Belgrade. Radovan Karadjic, the former president of Republica Srbska in Bosnia, who was wanted for the genocide of Muslims in Srebrenica, had lived for several years under the nose of the local authorities, enjoying their comfort, respect, and promise of security. He was even invited by different institutions to give lectures on mental health in auditoriums full of people. He wrote articles for a local magazine under the name of David Babic. He had changed his appearance very little. Goran Hadzic, a Serbian general from Croatia, and General Novak Dukic from Bosnia chose the capital of Serbia, Belgrade as a safe haven to hide out. My strong guess was that Dragan Spasic would continue to stay in Belgrade even after the clash with me in the hunting ground of the wild boars in Stara Planina.

"We don't have a photo of Daniel Krieger. There might be several individuals who might have the same first and last name like him in Perth. We have to check all of them one by one," I said with a note of pessimism in my voice.

"I have already searched through the internet links and came up with only three people who have the same name as Daniel Krieger. One of them is a photographer by profession and lives with his family in Freemantle in Western Australia. There are several photos of him which show that he is not our guy. The second is an American writer who lives in Japan, but goes back and forth to Perth. He has published his photos all over the place. The third Daniel Krieger has no photo."

"Third one might be our guy! Where does he live?"

"There's no information available on where this guy lives. Let's suppose that Dragan Spasic is using the fake identity of Daniel Krieger. What we know is that our 'Daniel' has to be a Serbian by nationality. It is natural that a Serbian fugitive outside Serbia would hide within the Serbian community in Perth. We have to conduct research on how many Serbian communities are in Perth. That is first. Another thing that we have to keep in our mind is the weakest point that 'our' Dragan has."

Arben paused a long time, until he got a reaction from me.

"What's his weakest point? What's your guess?"

My personal opinion was that Dragan Spasic didn't have any weak point. He was strong, intelligent and he was aware that we, the relatives of the victims, were after him.

Arben smiled and made a gesture with his finger as if he was pretending to open fire with a pistol. "He can't stop hunting wild boars! Hunting is deep in his veins. It's some kind of addiction, the same as a gambler who can't stop playing, even if he knows that he might lose all his life savings. The same as a drinker who is addicted to his vodka or Heineken. Addiction is like a disease that no one can escape, unless someone is supervising him strongly, babysitting him not to make a mistake. I really hope that he will not handle his addiction carefully and will start hunting his wild boars again. By nature, the human being finds it very hard to change old passions as they get older, and Dragan is around fifty. He might fight with himself at the beginning, but he will give up in the end and let himself slide toward his wild passion to shoot something."

"I hope he does. That 'Daniel' without the photo must be our Dragan," I said emotionally. "When should I fly straight to Australia?" I asked him. I had a yearning to get on the plane as soon as possible.

"There are a few things we have to keep in mind. I don't think you need to change your identity this time. Your own Canadian passport will help you travel to the destination as an ordinary tourist. The problem is how you are going to approach him, but let's go one step at a time. Make a list of all the Serbian localities in Perth first. Call me again when you're ready." Arben shut off his camera and exited Skype.

I didn't have time to fool around. I searched online for all the Serbian community centers in Perth. My eyes caught an interesting address: 498 Kenwick Rd, Maddington WA 6109. I printed out the information, folded the paper and placed it on my desk. I had to call a travel agency for a return ticket to Western Australia, but I didn't rush. First I stepped back a little and focused on the details of a plan. Hundreds of questions rose in my troubled mind. What was my purpose in going to Perth? If I saw Dragan, should I just jump on him and take him hostage? And take him where? Let's say I was able to take him to the Australian police, then what? What if he found a good lawyer and was released from detention and I went to jail for kidnapping instead?

There were some new challenges involved in my trip. This time there was no more Kosovo right beside the border where I could take Dragan if I succeeded in nabbing him. It was going to be a success only if I was able to collect some information from him as to where the mass grave was. Dragan was the only person who knew the whereabouts of the remains of my mother and my three little sisters. Another question I had to ask myself was what I was going to use as a cover? How could I reach him if he was pretending to be a priest in a local Serbian Orthodox church, or if he was an active member of the Serbian community center there? Was I going to be a hunter myself, with a rifle on my shoulder? Of course I needed a rifle, but if so then it was going to be assigned under the same fake name I used in Serbia, Bogdan Tadic. I already had a hunting permit under that name, as well as a hunting certificate under that name, so it should not be a problem for me to get a rifle in Australia. I just needed to show them my fake passport that I would also take with me, along with the original one. Time was ticking away and Dragan could go further into hiding if I waited until I got my hunting permit and a gun under my real name. The only changes I needed were the blue contact lenses and the colour of my hair.

If I needed to go straight to the Serbian Community Center in Maddington, I had to take a camera with me and pretend to be a photographer. I probably had to carry my fake plastic ID, under an assumed name. I kept planning, figuring out all the answers to possible issues that may come up, until past midnight, but nothing was sounding like a good plan. I felt my head get heavy and soon I fell asleep.

* * * *

Son! You are not going there alone! Can you hear me? If you really want to catch him, you have to go there with Babi and your cousin Arben. It doesn't matter for me anymore where my remains are. Dirt is dirt everywhere, my son! I am not too worried if my bones rest in a hole with no name, or in a beautiful grave covered with white marble tiles. The only thing I care for in this other life is You! I want you to be safe, no matter what you do; I don't want you to risk even a strand of your hair. Is it worth it to bring my remains home when you might lose your life out there? I am dead anyway, and I don't want in any circumstances that you should die looking for me. There are many other souls here, but none of us will rest in peace, if you, the living ones, suffer so much to find us. Forget about us! Earth belongs to earth; ashes to ashes and dust to dust!

* * * *

I woke up to a signal coming from Skype. I splashed cold water over my face, but the ghost of my mother was still inside my head.

The signal from Skype kept sounding, reminding me that the

caller was not giving up. I went back online. Arben understood from my frowning face that something was wrong, but he didn't ask me, hoping I could talk first. He saluted me like it wasn't just a few hours before that we spoke, but several weeks ago.

"I found the address of the Serbian community center in Maddington," I said and sighed deeply. "I think I have to go there, before he disappears again. First I am going to explore the center as a photographer who is interested in learning about the Serbian culture. Then I'll see what I can do. What do you think about that idea?"

Arben didn't seem happy either. He rubbed his chin, deep in thought.

"Not a good one! Interpol is supposed to do this, but Kosovo is not a member of this organization. I entered the Interpol website, but there is not even a single request for extradition for the war criminals who committed horrible crimes in Kosovo," Arben said.

I nodded and stared at him, waiting for his opinion.

"Okay, you said that my idea is not good. What's your idea?"

"I have a Swiss passport, so I'll meet you there in Perth."

"What about my father? Is he coming with us?" I asked him. Arben smiled a little and sighed deeply.

"We can't avoid him, can we? Of course he's coming with us. This is the very last chance to catch Dragan Spasic dead or alive. I will let you know about the details when we meet in Perth, in Western Australia," Arben said, as I heard my father knocking on the door.

"Hold on! Babi is here," I yelled.

Babi gave me a high five and sat in front of the computer. They talked to each other.

The ghost of my mother in my head was telling me that it was better if the three of us went to Perth in Western Australia. Otherwise Dragan Spasic could have a lot of unpleasant surprises waiting for us. I sat in front of my own laptop and used an online calculator. The total flight duration from Toronto to Perth, Australia was twenty-three hours. This was assuming an average flight speed for a commercial airliner of 500 mph, which was equivalent to 805 km/h or 434 knots. The calculator was also adding an extra thirty minutes for take-off and landing. I slapped my face struggling to focus, and finally made up my mind. It was going to be a very long trip indeed.

TWENTY-SIX

I stayed for two days in a hotel in Perth with my father, until Arben Morina arrived from Kosovo. Then the three of us rented a car and drove straight to Maddington. There we rented a van on Sampson Street, which was pretty close to Albany Highway. The company "Our Car Autos" had a twenty-dollar per day special for the weekend. I dropped off my dad and Arben at 75 Belmont Road at Belinda's Lunch Bar, which was only six minutes' drive from the Serbian center, and took the Honda Civic to 498 Kenwick Road. They were going to wait there until I was done with my reconnaissance of the Serbian center. I had a hunting gun in my trunk, which I got from Maverick Hunting Products in Perth.

It was late on Saturday night and a wedding party was taking place at the Serbian Cultural Center. There was a huge crowd of well-dressed people milling about. The men wore black suits and the women looked as if they were competing with each other on who wore the most attractive and colourful dress. I felt timid as I stepped into the corridor of the center. I noticed a few paintings on the walls. They showed aspects of the ordinary life of the Serbian peasant. I saw some similarities with the life of the Albanian shepherds on the mountains and the valleys of Albania.

At the end of the corridor, a few steps from the main entrance of the banquet hall, there was a small bar where a pretty bartender was serving cold drinks and little shots and beer to the guests. I approached the bar, watching the new faces entering the banquet hall where the dining tables were still awaiting guests. I downed a *Slivovica* shot in one breath and felt more at ease. I had a camera with me and a plastic ID with my picture, which was hanging from my white shirt pocket. The name on the ID card identified me as "Ben Miller." I had grown a little beard and I was wearing transparent eye glasses.

The sound of an old Slavic folk song filled the air. It was going to be difficult for me to get into the banquet hall without an invitation by the bride. Perhaps by standing at the bar, I would have a chance to study the guests. One of them came very close to me, holding the invitation to the wedding in his hand. I glanced at it from the corner of my eye. A young Macedonian man, Lubo Belisanec, was getting married to Jelena Gjokic, a Serbian girl. Her last name "Gjokic" reminded me that even today there are some Albanian families with the last name of "Gjoka." Before the Ottoman occupation of the Balkans, many Catholic Albanians used to get married to their Serbian neighbours.

As I was worrying about how to get into the banquet hall, my eyes caught the pretty face of a young woman. She was tall like me and had deep blue eyes. Her curly blonde hair made me flush feverishly. I had a sense that I knew the girl. I had seen her in my early childhood. I turned my head to the opposite side as I felt my heart pumping against my chest. It wasn't possible! There was no way that she was Slavica, my beautiful neighbour, the only daughter of Dragan Spasic. Perhaps I was experiencing some kind of hallucination created by my tired brain. I pretended I was interested in a painting that showed some Serbian shepherds herding a flock of sheep. This time I ordered a bottle of Heineken, turning my back to the corridor where the guests were coming in and out. In a moment or so I heard the swishing of a dress and a sweet female voice.

"Can I have a coke?" a young lady asked the bartender. She stood on my left. I noticed Slavica with the corner of my eye and shivered along my spine. What the hell did she want far away from Serbia? If she was married as her father Dragan had said, then why did she come alone to the southern continent of Australia? I guessed that if this lady was Slavica, then there was no doubt that her father Dragan was here as well with the new identity "Daniel Krieger." If Slavica recognized me, then I was going to be in danger again.

I decided to slink away. As soon as I took the first step toward the exit, a delicate hand touched me on the shoulder.

"Good evening! Are you the wedding photographer?" she asked me. Her smile created two little dimples on her cheeks. I was a hundred per cent sure that it was Slavica Spasic. A fever suffused my whole body.

"No, but I am interested in learning about the Serbian

culture. But I'm here now just in case someone needs another photographer. It happens in big events like this, you know," I said to her, avoiding any unnecessary eye contact.

"I know!" Slavica said. "Nice meeting you! Your name is...?"

"Ben... Ben Miller."

"My name is Slavica."

"I know who you are!" I almost declared to her, but kept quiet instead. She extended her hand toward me, which I squeezed gently. Her fingers were long, thin and soft. Was she good at playing the piano, I wondered? The very white colour of her skin and the smell of her perfume made the blood pump deep in my veins. The Kosovars say that "you can never find an ugly Serbian woman!"

"Do I know you? I am afraid that I met you somewhere," she asked me, and I noticed a vibration in her voice.

"I don't think so. You've probably mixed me up with somebody else." I was short and sharp in my answer. I could never cherish feelings for a woman whose father killed most of the members of my family and wiped out several Albanian neighbourhoods.

"Why don't you hang around, just in case. I am sure we might need more than one photographer for our wedding. Please follow me," she said and turned her back, heading to the entrance of the banquet hall.

"Okay! I appreciate that," I said in a cool voice and followed her.

The dining tables were huge and could easily fit eight guests. Slavica pointed her finger toward one of the tables which was set not too far from the entrance, on which a notice with the word "Guests" was placed, and invited me with a sweet smile to sit there. I cleared my throat shyly, as if I was attempting to get rid of the fear and the emotions that were coming together like a ball in my throat.

"You can sit here anytime you want to take a break or if you feel you want to eat or drink something." Slavica stared at me for a second, still wondering if she met me somewhere. Even though I had grown a mustache and beard, my face looked very familiar to Slavica, but thank God she didn't realize yet that it was me, the Albanian boy Ermal who really liked her when we were preteens. In order to avoid her drilling look, I got to my feet and pretended that I was checking the camera.

"I am okay right now. I better take some shots," I said, chuckling a little. As soon as I took the first photo, Slavica waved at me "goodbye" and disappeared into the crowd. I heard an old Slavic song, as the guests got up from their table one after another, forming a circle in the middle of the hall, and started to dance, holding hands. One step, two, three... There were so many similarities between their folk dance and the Albanian one.

I searched the farthest corners of the banquet hall, but Dragan Spasic was nowhere to be found. There were more than two hundred guests in the hall, but none of them looked like Dragan. Two waiters carried a roasted boar on a huge tray, passing by every single table for people to serve themselves. When the waiters stopped at my table, I took a piece of meat from the roasted boar and threw a bunch of Australian dollars on the table. Leaving money on the tray was an Albanian tradition and I was not sure if it was a Serbian tradition as well, but most of the guests did the same. They filled the tray with money, whatever they had in their pockets. It was a mistake. Now I was at the epicenter of their attention. I was scared and tired and didn't know what to do.

I spotted Slavica. I got up from the table and followed her carefully as she went outside and got into a car. There were several cars parked in front of the banquet hall. I took my rental Honda civic and followed Slavica. We hadn't even driven ten kilometers away when Slavica deviated from the main highway and took a secondary road which ended at the front yard of a three-storey building. I didn't stop. I pretended that I was going somewhere on my own and turned back from a side road to Belinda's Lunch Bar, where my father and Arben were still waiting.

"Did you see him?" Arben asked me anxiously.

"I saw Slavica, his daughter. I followed her. Dragan Spasic is only ten kilometers away from here," I said and turned back to the car.

* * * *

I stood only a few steps away from Dragan Spasic with my gun pointing at the back of his head. My father Adem and cousin Arben were lying on the ground among the bushes, ready to intervene if I signaled them. I took a few more steps behind his back and spoke to him in a low voice.

"Don't move, Dragan! Put your gun down and turn around!"

Dragan was shocked for a moment, but he lay the gun down and turned around to face me. He lifted both his hands up in the air and looked at me with wonder, recognizing me in spite of my disguise.

"You found me even at this corner of the planet," he said with a note of despair in his voice.

"That's right!" I said, taking another step toward him. I noticed my father and Arben coming out of the bushes, holding knives in their hands. I kicked Dragan's gun as hard as I could, pushing it toward Arben, who grabbed it immediately and pointed it at Dragan as well. There were two barrels now pointing at Dragan's forehead. "Now tell us where you dumped the Albanian victims of Milos Gilica Street. Where is the mass grave?" I asked him, with my finger on the trigger. I stepped a little closer toward him.

"The grave is in a hilly, rural area of Rudnica, near the town of Raska, one hundred and eighty kilometers south of Belgrade," Dragan said in a low voice.

"Where exactly?" I asked him again. "Do you have any specific details?"

"There is a house and a small parking lot near a road nestled between the hills. The mass grave is located beneath the building and the parking lot," Dragan said, shaking with fright. "Is that what you want? I am so sorry, man! I don't know why we did this! But you have to understand that we had orders," he yelped, his eyes full of fear.

"You are not going to run anymore from justice. Here, take some memories with you," I said and shot him in both legs. The third bullet went to his hunting gun, which I destroyed.

Dragan started bleeding and yelling in Serbian. Slavica came out of the house, looking at us in horror. I didn't run. She didn't move either. I looked from her to her father and back to her. Finally, she realized who I was and why I didn't kill her father.

I looked at her for the last time and went back with Arben and Adem to the car, which I had parked on the road. Then we drove away.

www.ingramcontent.com/pod-product-compliance
Lightning Source LLC
Chambersburg PA
CBHW070628310726
48982CB00001B/199